WOLF
the journey home

WOLF
the journey home

'Asta Bowen

BLOOMSBURY

To Marta

Copyright © 1997, 2006 by 'Asta Bowen
Originally published as *Hungry for Home: A Wolf Odyssey* by Simon & Schuster in 1997

Published by Bloomsbury Publishing, New York, London, and Berlin
Distributed to the trade by Holtzbrinck Publishers

Library of Congress Cataloging-in-Publication Data
Bowen, 'Asta.
[Hungry for home]
Wolf : the journey home / 'Asta Bowen.
p. cm.
Originally published: Hungry for home. New York : Simon & Schuster, 1997.
ISBN-10: 1-58234-689-5 • ISBN-13: 978-1-58234-689-2 (hardcover : alk. paper)
1. Wolves—Fiction. 2. Montana—Fiction. 3. Wolves—Reintroduction—Fiction. 4. Canadian
Rockies (B.C. and Alta.)—Fiction. I. Bowen, 'Asta. Hungry for home. II. Title.
PS3552.O856H86 2006   813'.54—dc22   2005045212

Printed in the U.S.A.
1 3 5 7 9 10 8 6 4 2

Bloomsbury Publishing, Children's Books, U.S.A.
175 Fifth Avenue, New York, NY 10010

CONTENTS

Contents

PART THREE

Contents

PRONUNCIATION NOTE

Here are the local pronunciations of some words in this story. Vowel sounds are short unless otherwise specified.

Camas	CAM us
Chinook	shi NOOK
Evaro	EV a roh
Kootenai	KOOT nee
Ovando	o VAN doh
Tenino	ten NINE oh

PART ONE

ONE

the noise that changed everything

Marta was deep in the den nursing her pups when she heard it. One sharp crack, like a lone thunderbolt, pierced the clay roof and stung her ears. Oldtooth, asleep just outside the den, twitched and jerked awake, his worn face groggy for an instant, then alert.

Marta had heard this sound before, and it did not mean a storm. It meant trouble. She stood up in the darkness, and the newborns tumbled away from her. She crept to the mouth of the den and listened, her black fur glinting in the starlight that filtered through the trees. All was quiet. She sniffed.

With her great wolf nose, Marta sniffed again. She smelled the spring rain that had fallen the day before, and she smelled dogtooth violets in the meadow. She smelled thawing soil and budding trees, and she smelled

several fat mice within a quick pounce from the den—
but for once, the mice didn't tempt her.

She smelled the scent left by Calef, her mate, and it
told her how long he had been gone on the evening hunt.
She smelled a dull, oily haze from the road nearby, and
she smelled the remains of a recent meal, a snowshoe
hare Oldtooth had gotten all by himself. Then she
smelled it: clear as a stroke of lightning in the stillness,
the sting of gunpowder hit her nose, and every muscle
froze.

Marta's head filled with the smell, and her heart began to pound. She looked at Oldtooth, who had not gotten up but was still peering in the direction of the sound.
If the smell had reached him, he gave no sign.

Oldtooth did not move, and all was quiet again. The
stinging smell drifted past, and the new leaves around
the den stirred in the night air. Nothing but the mice
moved on the ground. Marta's heart finally steadied, and
the blood stopped pounding in her ears. Hearing the babies mewling in the blackness, she turned inside and
crawled back to them. At the inner chamber she stood
again for a moment, listening; then she nuzzled all three
pups close together, dropped her rear end, folded her
legs, and lay down to wait for Calef.

This was their first year on the Montana frontier, and
their first year together. The birth a few days before was

also their first. Marta had traveled far from the north to find this valley, to find Calef, to find her place in the world. It hadn't been easy.

It had not been easy in the north, either. Born last in her litter and never quite accepted by the pack, her first years were a struggle for food, for protection, and for learning the way of the wolf. The way of the wolf was ancient and wild, a code of survival more than a million years old. Taught by example from one generation to the next, it was a code of the pack that found strength in numbers; a code of hunting that killed without waste; a code of order in which every animal had its place.

In those days, Marta's place was on the fringes of the pack, and she had had to learn the way of the wolf from a distance. Being an outcast made her strong and taught her to survive on her own. Marta was, above all, a survivor.

Now for the first time she had a real pack, with Calef and Oldtooth and the little ones. She had a pack and a place in the world: a home.

Home. For Marta, as for any wild creature, habitat was everything, and Pleasant Valley was a good habitat for a wolf. Broad and sweeping, with miles of meadow surrounded by a sea of trees, the valley lay on the gentler side of the Rocky Mountains. Foothills and forests stretched for days in almost every direction, and toward the morning sun lay the backbone of the continent, guarded north and south by vast reaches of wilderness.

No wolves had settled in this valley for a long time. A thousand years ago, Marta's and Calef's ancestors had ranged across the continent, hunting and singing from one valley to the next. But those were the days when humans were few on the land and lived much as wolves did. Now the land was covered with a new kind of human, a loud and busy tribe that changed everything. They filled the prairies with buildings and roads. They drove the animals into the forest and cut down the forests. They turned rivers to lakes and lakes to rivers. They carved wide paths through the mountains and dug huge holes in the earth. They outshone the stars with their lights. And they killed.

They killed deer and bear and elk and buffalo. They killed moose and grouse and beaver. They killed salmon. They killed eagle. And they killed wolf.

In the old days, both wolves and humans killed in order to live, and both survived. But when the new humans came they killed in new ways, and much was wasted. Many wolves died and many more were driven out, and the last wolf homeland was pushed far to the north.

Since the new humans came, the forest wasn't safe. The earth itself sometimes grew teeth: sharp, strong ones. A wolf could be sniffing the mark of an intruder, trying to protect the pack's territory, and the ground could reach up and snap around its toes, and hold tighter and tighter until it never let go. Oldtooth knew about the metal bite. It had almost killed him once. Marta knew, too; she had watched from a distance as a packmate howled and thrashed to exhaustion, only to be carried away by a man. Humans made many dangers for wolves, especially young loners without the protection of the pack and the wisdom of their elders. Young loners like she had been.

Marta avoided humans. She learned to dodge their traps and cars and guns, and especially to dodge their scent. In Pleasant Valley the people were few and kept to their homes and ranches at the far end of the meadow. But wherever they went, they left their mark. Wherever they went, they brought loud noises and stinging smells like the one still lingering in Marta's nose and mind.

That night, Calef was slow to return. As the leaves whispered outside and the stars wheeled overhead, Marta waited. Perhaps he was taking extra time to get the best kill; the babies, it seemed, changed everything. He had never been gone this long before.

In the darkness of the den, she and the little ones were safe. She felt three soft, round noses and paws searching the skin of her belly where it was stretched full of milk. Marta could not see them in the darkness, but she did not have to. Knowing each pup by its smell, she felt the gray female, then the black male, and finally the little black female find a nipple and begin to pull. Marta curled around them, making a warm circle in the dark, and listened as they nursed themselves to sleep.

When light finally came and the first birds rustled awake, Calef still had not returned. Marta left the pups sleeping with Oldtooth at the door of the den and set out to find her mate. She dropped her head and let the scent of his tracks fill her nose, drawing a map of the path he had taken.

Trotting up the hill behind the den, she noticed one of Calef's long guard hairs caught on the bare branch of a shrub. At the top of the ridge she stepped over a fresh dung pile of his, squatted to mark it, and continued down the tunnel of his scent. His tracks dropped gradually over the other side, crossing and recrossing game trails and creek beds still filled with snow. Soon the trail led toward a human place, where the trees had been cut down and replaced with buildings and roads and animals behind fences: not wolf, not elk, not deer, not bear. Something small and white and woolly and slow.

As Marta drew near she trotted more softly, pausing now and then to lift her head and listen. All was quiet except for the sleepy bleating of the sheep and their young. She was almost to the fence line when she stopped dead. The smell of blood filled her head. Ten feet away she saw the awful truth: grasses battered flat by hard, human footprints and soaked with patches of thickening blood. Calef's blood.

Marta's senses exploded. Calef was hurt! Where was he? She circled the beaten grasses, first left, then right, then left again, but found no more tracks. She circled, stopped, and sniffed the air: nothing. Circled back and stopped. Impossible. The trail ended here, in this troubled patch of meadow grass. Marta's head felt huge and thick, a dead weight on her neck. A trace of the gun smell that had come in the night hovered over the grass, and her great nose sagged.

No Calef. Just his scent, still fresh, long flecks of his gray fur, and too much blood. No sign of the brushy tail that waved high when they played. No clever eyes, no soft ears, no strong muzzle that could crush the haunch of a deer in one motion.

Marta's throat closed. The sound, the smell, the blood all fit together now and meant one thing. Calef. Gone.

She stood for a long moment in the morning light, poised at the spot where her mate's trail ended. Then she huffed, a great snort that seemed to come from her heart instead of her lungs, turned, and ran low and fast all the way back to the den.

TWO

oldtooth's arithmetic

Oldtooth had planted himself firmly in front of the den when Marta left to look for Calef and was still on alert when he heard her coming back through the trees. His teeth were old but his nose was wise, and the stinging smell that came in the night had troubled both his sleep and his waking. It was the smell of death, and when he saw Marta returning alone, tail low and eyes dim, he knew. Calef was gone.

Calef was gone, and Oldtooth's ears sagged. Wolves have their own arithmetic, and they know it by heart. Oldtooth had lived through seven winters so far, three of them as the alpha male leading his own pack. In those three years, he and his mate birthed litters of two, then ten, then six, and raised them with the help of other adults in the pack. As the young grew, they either joined the group as hunters or went off on their own. Of eighteen births, only seven lived long enough to stay or go. Though bad weather and disease took a few and a mountain lion got another, the greatest threat was starvation.

A well-fed wolf could usually escape from danger and disease; a hungry wolf lived next to death. Oldtooth had been a youngster once, and a hungry one. Born in a summer of drought, he was weaned at a dry nipple and learned to fight for scraps of meat and bone. Most of his littermates starved.

Later, when he and his mate had their own pack, they had to know when to hunt and when to rest, where to travel and what dangers to avoid. Only they would breed and bear the pack's young, and when strange wolves approached, they decided who was welcome and who was not.

As the alpha, Oldtooth learned the signs that would spell life or death for his pack. He could read the numbers of deer in the layers of winter snow and the size of buds in spring. In good seasons and bad, he knew how much meat three big healthy wolves could get and how much three small hungry ones could eat. In this pack he was not the leader, and he was no longer strong. Calef was the alpha male, and he was dead. That left Marta, the alpha female, and Oldtooth: one and a half healthy adults to feed themselves and three hungry youngsters.

The old wolf's eyes softened. He looked toward the den, toward Marta and the pups, and it added up to one thing. He looked toward the forest, toward the many deer it would take to feed them, and it added up to another. Finally he looked at his own ragged paws and felt a hollow stab in his belly: it was the old drought, echoing down the years.

But there was no drought now. In fact, Oldtooth's belly was nicely rounded. He and Calef and Marta had eaten well all winter, having had a fine meal just a few days ago in a yearling doe they had hunted together. With the meat from his latest hare, Oldtooth still felt a certain fullness between his ribs.

That fullness would not last. The hunger would start in his stomach and travel outward. In a few days it would seep through his bones, into his muscles and under his skin, and spread up the ridge to his tail, making it twitch. Next it would shoot down to his paws, bringing him to his feet, then crawl up his throat like a howl and end in his mouth, sending a sharp command to his teeth.

His teeth. What Oldtooth lacked, and what his instinct and experience could not replace, was the most basic hunting tool: sharp, strong teeth. When still the alpha of his old pack, he was caught in a metal trap, a small trap meant for coyotes. Rather than break off his leg, he chewed through the steel. It took a long time, but more importantly, it took his teeth. Now Oldtooth's front teeth were worn in half, and others were ground to the bone; where Marta had fangs that could pierce through wood, he had rounded nubs that didn't even touch.

He still had enough teeth to eat small amounts of meat, but not enough to take down a deer or elk on the run. Smaller animals he could kill with pressure from his jaws, and in desperate times, he had taken some small steers. It wasn't his first choice of food, and in Pleasant Valley he had never touched the range cattle, but these were good times—or had been, until now.

Without Calef, there would be no more hunts like the one a few days ago. It was one of those calm spring days when the snow crystals grow fat and glossy, sparkling from the tips of tree branches. The pups were not born yet, and Marta's sides swelled with their weight. She had just finished digging the den, and all three wolves were napping in the late afternoon sun when Calef signaled the time to hunt. He woke Marta first. Standing in front of her, he wore the hunting face and whined the hunting whine.

Marta was on her feet in an instant, belly low, and swung her tail from side to side as they locked eyes. She was hungry, too. She licked and nipped at Calef's muzzle, the traditional wolf kiss, and he licked and nipped back until the kiss turned playful, a mock tussle with much growling and clashing of teeth. Suddenly Calef opened his jaws, tipped back his massive head, and began to howl. When Marta joined in, their singing woke Oldtooth and brought him to his feet. He added a third voice to the chorus, and nose to nose they sang their food-finding song. One by one their voices trailed away, and they stood wagging tails as the notes threaded off into the trees. This was the way of the wolf.

Oldtooth, who had the most experience in choosing prey, pointed the way; his pace was slow, but his instinct was sure. He led downhill from the den site, pausing at the road that circled the valley. Few cars came this way, but when they did, the wolves had to hide and wait for them to pass. That day the road lay damp and undisturbed in the sun. Nothing more than a badger had been by, though the clay was plotted with droppings from the cattle that shared the valley floor.

Marta's nose wrinkled at the smell. Unlike deer pellets, cow piles were sloppy, stinking messes. Even as an outcast, Marta had learned which animals were food and which were not. Deer were always food; elk and moose were food if a pack could catch them. Smaller animals like rabbit and beaver were easy prey for a lone wolf.

Bears were not food, and neither were lions. Birds and fish were sometimes food, but usually not.

Cows, which arrived shortly after the new kind of humans, didn't fit in. They walked on four legs and chewed cud like deer, but their hides were thick and their bones were immense. They didn't smell or act like anything else in the forest, and they made hideous noises for no reason at all. Like other things connected with people, Marta avoided them.

Following Oldtooth's nose, the wolves crossed the road. With one eye toward food and the other toward danger, they ran single file along the meadow's edge until they were across from the lake. Then they darted across the grass to a stand of tall aspen trees at the water's edge.

From the shelter of the aspens, they could survey much of the valley with its wooded hills on either side. The landscape was still in winter drab, but sunlight caught on the first sprigs of green. Deer tracks crisscrossed the meadow, radiating from the lake into the surrounding forest. Oldtooth had a second sense about deer tracks; from pellets alone, he could tell which animals were old or ill. From hoofprints, he could tell which were lame. Keeping near the fringe of the aspens, he sniffed delicately at one trail and then another. Marta and

Calef followed, checking the signs Oldtooth checked and ignoring the ones he ignored.

Suddenly, the old wolf's pace quickened. Ears forward, eyes narrow, his nose dropped to the ground and didn't come up again. He began to run. Now it was Marta's turn, and she took up the scent: it was of a young doe, medium size, with an odd tinge to its leavings. Marta trotted out ahead and began to pick up speed.

Marta was strong on the hunt. Where Calef was solid and Oldtooth shrewd, she was fast, with endurance to spare. Her eyes glowed gold as she led into the sun, and silver lights flickered in her black fur. Fine-boned and lean, the weight of pregnancy slowed her now, but nothing stopped her. She loved the chase.

Where the scent was strong, Marta sprinted; where it grew faint, she slowed. Oldtooth dropped to the rear and loped behind Calef at a steady rate. The scent of food filled their noses, and blood began to sing in their ears. Hearts pounded, tongues panted, and a tingle started at the base of their teeth. Marta led them out of the meadow and across the road—this time, no one stopped to listen—and into a draw west of the new den.

In the underbrush, Marta slowed. Her padded feet fell silently through the kinnikinnick, over fallen timber, and around stumps. Up the hill the scent grew stronger and fresher, but the wolves neither howled nor whined their excitement. A young doe could run, and fast; silence was essential for surprise.

Suddenly a flash caught Marta's eye: the whitetail. Startled, Marta stepped hard on a branch, which gave way with a snap. Up jerked the deer's head, and she spun around and saw the wolves: three sets of teeth and tongue panting toward her on a run. Tail high, with a spray of pellets the deer bounded away.

The surprise lost, Marta tore through the trees. Crushing branches and breaking brush, she squeezed the heat from her muscles for a full sprint, testing the deer. Had the doe won that race, Marta would have stopped, signaling an end to the chase and saving the pack's energy for easier prey. But the deer lagged, and the wolves gained on her.

When Marta was almost at the doe's tail, she lunged. It was a takedown move, aimed for the side of the belly, but could be deadly either way. An error here, and the wolf could catch a flying hoof in her face, taking out an eye or even precious teeth. But the timing was right, and Marta's jaws met flesh. A bite, a twist, and the hide tore open.

The deer did not stop, racing now against the loss of her own blood. From the side Marta lunged again, missed and fell back. Normally she would have made the strike, but the weight in her belly cost her the span of a tooth. Before Marta could catch her breath for another try, Calef soared over her back, landing square in the path of the deer. She reared up, spinning away, but there was Oldtooth: paws forward, head lowered, staring her down with huge eyes. Cornered, the deer twisted back again, but Calef twisted with her. He spun in midair, jaws wide, and connected with her throat. For an instant, the shadow of his enormous head fell across her neck. Then a sinking bite, a crush, and the deer fell. The chase was done.

Calef and Marta tore into the animal, with Oldtooth close behind. The meat was lean and healthy, except for a milky place in the gut that smelled like the tinge in her droppings. Avoiding that place, ripping hide and gulping flesh, the pack fed until they could eat no more. Then they rested, cleaning themselves as ravens circled in on the remains.

Oldtooth blinked. That was three days ago. There would be no more such hunts now that Calef was gone. Without Calef, their hunting team was down to two; with the new litter of pups, their numbers were up to five. As long as the babies were too young to be left alone, both adults could not hunt at once, and the team went from two to one. That one, because of Oldtooth's condition, had to be Marta. Unfortunately, it was also

Marta who carried the milk to nurse the babies. The burden of the pack's survival fell on her narrow black shoulders.

Oldtooth did his arithmetic. He measured himself and Marta against the deer they would need every week to survive. He measured the pups beginning to toddle about inside the den, and pictured them in autumn: one would survive. With luck, good weather, and easy hunting, two might make it—but not three. Not without Calef. It just didn't add up.

THREE

a baby's cry

Fortunately for the wolves, winter ended kindly that year. The first rains were generous, rushing down the creeks to water the great basin of Pleasant Valley. The edges of Dahl Lake sparkled as it filled and spread toward the aspen grove. New meadow grasses wiggled up through the old, and the deer of Pleasant Valley gave birth to more fawns than usual. The herd grazed everywhere, even in the meadow near the wolf den.

In the days after the pups' birth and Calef's death, Marta scarcely left the den. On his own, Oldtooth did the only kind of hunting he could, snatching every rabbit, mouse, mole, and vole in his path and making short work of one fawn left untended by its mother. One day he even stalked a badger, but all he got for his pains was a badger bite. Not all animals are easy victims, even for a wolf, and when Oldtooth slunk back to the den, he turned to hide the notch in his fur.

Marta did not notice his slinking, and she did not notice the notch. Despite the gifts of food Oldtooth presented at the door of the den, despite the signs of an easy spring, despite her three new pups, Marta suffered the loss of her mate.

Her eyes and fur seemed flat, and she carried her tail low. Nursing took all her energy; she did not hunt and she did not play. Before, the simplest acts of waking up, chewing a stick, or even grooming could turn into a game on a moment's notice. But since Calef's death, neither Oldtooth nor Marta had worn a play face or whined a play whine.

The burden of survival fell to Marta, and for now, it fell heavily. The first task, nursing the pups, occupied her entirely. For several weeks she did not hunt, living on whatever Oldtooth could bring her. She did not leave the pups except to drink—making short trips to the creek—and to relieve herself. There was one exception. Every night, just as Calef had done on his last hunt, Marta slipped from the den after sundown. Leaving Oldtooth on guard, she put her nose to the ground and followed her mate's last trail, returning night after night to the same place: the ridge top above the den.

At the crest of the hill she stopped, sniffed the air,

and whined softly, swishing her tail in the dusk. The wind blew darkness into her black fur, and the steep angles of her face faded into the night. Sometimes her whine grew louder, filling her throat like a groan, and she would lift her great nose to the sky, blinking as the whine became a howl. Sometimes high, sometimes low; sometimes soft, sometimes loud; she sang the ache in her belly and the hollow in her chest. She sang the hungry song, the lonesome song, the lost song, and the song that only she and Calef knew.

Her howls echoed to the south, making the sheep look up from their beds. They echoed to the north, rolling down tops of trees and fading over the meadow. Sometimes a trickle of sound reached all the way into the den, where three sightless pups huddled on the clay and whimpered to each other, not knowing why. When Marta returned, they tumbled over one another in a rush to her warmth.

One morning when the babies were a few weeks old, Marta was awakened by a tiny cry. She nuzzled at her belly and found only the two larger pups curled there. Sula, the black female and smallest of the three, was missing. Once their eyes opened, the pups had begun to explore the den, so Marta sniffed expectantly for the little one. But Sula was not exploring; she had dragged herself off to the edge of the den, where there was nothing but cold and clay. Marta made a long reach with her head, bared her front teeth, and grasped Sula by the skin of the neck, drawing her daughter close. Something was wrong.

Marta sniffed intently at the pup, front to back. The little one was trembling and cold, but her tiny nose was hot. Her breath came short and dry at the mouth, and she was dry at the rear too. All three babies were still scruffy and rat-tailed, but where her brother and sister, Rann and Annie, were round, she was flat.

Sula's problem was simple but deadly: she was starving. Her brother and sister were quicker to nurse and stronger to suck, and when Marta's milk ran out—as it too often did—Sula was the one who went hungry.

In the blackness, Marta's ears went forward. The hair went up on her neck, and she nosed Rann and Annie roughly away. Ignoring their squeals, she pushed Sula to the front, the fullest teat, and nudged the pup's dry nose toward it. Then Marta waited. Sula blinked, sniffing weakly about her, not realizing where she was. Her little head wobbled when she finally smelled milk, but she didn't open her mouth. Marta pressed out a droplet and guided Sula to it.

When her lips touched milk, Sula finally opened her mouth and closed it around the nipple. Marta felt a slight pull. Sula swallowed a few drops and stopped. Marta whined, touching Sula's cheek with her nose, and the infant sucked again, stronger this time. When she swallowed again, Rann and Annie wiggled closer for their share, but Marta gave the softest of warnings—not a growl, but a coarse breath from deep in her throat—and the two backed away. Sula nursed fitfully, and by the time Marta felt her milk finally begin to flow, Rann and Annie had fallen asleep in the warmth of her lower belly. After a time, Sula's sucking slowed and then stopped. Marta heard the tiniest of sighs and felt the infant's mouth slide from her nipple. Sula, too, was asleep.

Marta laid her nose on her paws. Eyes wide and ears pricked, she listened to the breathing of her young. The time had come. When they wakened, she would hunt.

FOUR

last in line

Marta had not had to hunt alone, not for anything more than beaver, since meeting up with Calef. Alone was how she had learned to hunt, back in the north; that time was dim now, far in the past, though it had been little more than a year since she lost her birth pack. Marta drew a long breath. Those were not the good old days. Not at all.

She watched Sula sleeping and lapped at the moisture that began to trickle, finally, from under the pup's tail. Marta had been last in her litter too—but she had had six brothers and sisters, not two. The year she was born there was plenty of wild game, and the pack had plenty of adults to feed her nursing mother. Still, with seven noses scrambling for a teat, when the milk was gone, it was gone. Marta had never been as thin as Sula—but never as plump as Rann or Annie, either.

From the time Marta was born, she was forced to the outside, the back, the end of the line and beyond. When the pups left the den, she was the last one out. When the pack moved for the first time, she was barked back and had to follow at a distance. When she finally caught up at the rendezvous site, she watched from the edge of the clearing as her brothers and sisters licked at the mouths of their elders. Her mouth watered when the adults heaved up the meat they had carried back from the kill site in their bellies.

When Marta couldn't hold back any longer, she moved in. Braving snarls and snaps, she darted after scraps missed by the others. She picked up bones her siblings dropped, and ran away to chew them clean. But if she tried to whine or lick for her own food, most of the adults turned their muzzles away. A few growled outright. As time went on, Marta discovered one pack member—an older female with eyes like Oldtooth's—who would give what she had. But by the time Marta could get near, there was not much to be given.

Now, years later, Marta's own daughter was struggling for life, not because Sula was an outcast but because one of the pack's hunters had been killed. Though Oldtooth tried, he could not bring back enough meat to feed Marta and the new pups, not to mention himself. Half a hunter could not feed a whole pack; his arithmetic held true.

When Annie wakened from her nap, she wriggled in and began to nurse. Marta did not stop her this time, but nudged Sula too. The black eyes did not open, and Marta nudged harder, heart pumping—and the pup blinked awake. With another touch from her mother's nose, she parted her tiny jaws and fastened them to the nipple.

Rann, the plumpest of the three, skipped mealtime to inspect the new order of things in the den. He toddled a few steps from Marta's thin hindquarters and sniffed at Sula as she drank. The tip of his black tail waved in the darkness, and he moved on toward Marta's head. There he received an affectionate lick, which became a thorough cleaning. With a few swats at Marta's nose and cheeks, Rann tried to turn the bath to playtime, but his mother ignored the bats from his puppy paws. As soon as he was clean, she sent him off with a gentle push to his backside.

There would be no playtime today, because the time had come for Marta to hunt. Sula was alert now, but her breathing came short and shallow. The others would be fine for a few hours; Annie had finished nursing and was already trading puppy snarls and neck attacks with

Rann. As for Sula—if Marta was gone too long, the pup might die. But if Marta did not go now, she would certainly die. The milk was gone, and the ache in Marta's belly had begun to chafe at her ribs. Marta gently pushed the pup from her belly. Giving Sula a long look and a short, earnest lick, she ducked out through the den tunnel.

Outside, Marta blinked at the brightness of the day. Oldtooth had been listening, chin on paws, to Rann and Annie playing inside, and looked up in surprise when Marta stepped over the pair of squirrels he had laid at the den entrance. Then he saw the reason: for the first time since the pups were born, she was wearing the hunting face.

Hunger showed in the hollows under her eyes, and her narrow form seemed even narrower. Her coat looked shaggy, more gray than black, but her eyes burned bright as sulphur. Oldtooth rose to his feet. In Marta's face he saw the promise of food and licked her whiskers with a graceful sweep. Then the two stood, nose to nose, and sang a hunting song. Now the sole alpha of their small pack, Marta held her head high, sweeping her tail in broad strokes as Calef had always done.

Then she was off.

FIVE

marta hunts alone

This hunt had to be fast and sure. The sun already shone high above the east hills, and before it slanted far to the west, Marta would have to be back at the den with meat in her belly. Energized by Oldtooth's salute and the pang under her ribs, she headed toward the road.

Midday was not the best time for hunting. Deer liked to bed down during the bright hours, coming out early or late. But this was Pleasant Valley; the animals were everywhere, and Marta would find one. Five lives depended on it.

Seeing nothing in the meadow, Marta turned and trotted down the road. This was one rule of wolf travel: never go the hard way if there's an easy one. She ran with purpose, stepping around the cow piles that, though dry, still rankled her nose. Other scents that rose from the clay made her move quickly along the road: oil and metal. Metal and oil, the smell of humans.

Marta had barely begun to pant when the first hint of food hit her nostrils. She took a long drink of the smell as Oldtooth always did, but all she could tell was that the tracks were fresh. She dropped her head to follow them, but jerked it back up at a puff of air from the trees.

The scent said there was a large, warm animal on the hillside. Deer or elk, young or old, it was food and it was close. Marta sniffed the air casually. She made no sound as she slipped off the road and into the barrow pit. Like a sculpture she froze there, pointed uphill: ears forward, legs rigid, only the tiny muscles around her nose trembling. The air was full of new ferns, lichen, kinnikinnick sprouts, rotting logs—but only one scent mattered. Food. The message spread from her nose to her lungs, pumping blood to her muscles and out to the roots of her guard hairs. The black mane around her neck stood out straighter. Her teeth tingled.

Suddenly the air overhead broke with a blast of sound, and Marta dropped. The grass was too short for cover, so she flattened herself in the ditch and cringed against the roar of an engine. As the mud seeped through her thin fur, an airplane appeared, buzzing the hillside. Marta eased deeper into the chill, waiting for the noise of the plane to fade. When she stood again, she could not tell if the animal she had scented was still there.

Marta shook off the cold and crept into the trees. Her casual air was gone, and the fearful triangle of her eyes and nose focused on one thing. Directly ahead, in a shallow between two fir trees, were two tips of velvet. Buck velvet. Not five lengths away, a whitetail deer was down for a midday rest. Marta had never chanced this close to sleeping prey. She took a step, feeling the downhill flow of air that was keeping her wolf scent away from him.

Marta inched closer, and his ears did not flicker. Finding bare soil, the most silent footing, she stepped carefully around each twig and leaf. She placed one footpad to the earth, and then the other. Pad, earth. Pad, earth. The antler tips did not move. Marta moved on instinct: breathe deep. No scent. Move swiftly. No sound. Fill lungs and prepare to kill. If her body was drained from nursing, her instinct was not.

Two lengths away from the antlers, she lunged. With a thrust from her haunches, she flew teeth first over the rise, aiming at an unseen spot under the tips of velvet. When she closed her mouth, it was filled with blood. But she had hit the shoulder instead of the neck, and the buck jerked awake, punching a velvet spike into her side. Marta flinched, but the new antler was still soft, and did not hurt her. She bit harder, tearing his hide open. More blood. The buck speared her again. She let go, gave desperate aim at the windpipe, and bit. The buck stiffened, then slumped.

Now Marta tore back the hide, gulping neck meat, veins, and tendons in one mouthful. Next she opened the belly, taking the first strips of summer fat. Soon she was bathed in blood. It soaked her jaws and paws, and flecked her black coat as she took organ from muscle and muscle from bone. She savored the softest parts first, leaving less to spoil, and paused only to listen, catch her breath, or swallow a string of intestine. As she ate, a lone raven appeared and circled overhead, landing on a high branch and clucking over the kill.

Before long Marta's stomach, shrunken from weeks of small meals, began to protest. She could hold no more. When the pups were older, she could put more in her belly, since it would only be full while she carried the meat back to them. For now, her system still had to turn it into milk. Marta's gulps slowed, then stopped. She sniffed the length of the carcass, licking at the rich blood. Then she went to work on her fur, cleaning her face, paws, and the body of her coat.

Drowsiness set in as she cleaned herself, lulled by the strokes of her tongue. Her eyelids sagged and her neck bent in the afternoon sun, now slanting over the trees to the west. Marta's cleaning slowed, then stopped. Her head nodded and hung still. When she heard a howl, she could not tell if it was a dream or real, but it was Oldtooth's call, and it woke her with a start. Sula! The pups needed her immediately. Marta struggled to her feet, surprising the ravens who had arrived to pluck at the kill. Stopping at the creek, she drank until her sides ached from the strain. Then she trudged toward the den site, heavy with fatigue and the weight in her belly.

Oldtooth, who had not budged from the entrance to the den, greeted her with a wilder version of the hunting salute he gave when she left. Despite her grooming, she still smelled fabulously of fresh blood, and he licked at her muzzle. As she would for an older pup, Marta heaved up a token of the meat for him so that he could follow her steps back to the open carcass and feed for himself. As Oldtooth gobbled down the meat, blinking gratefully, Marta gave her coat a last cleaning. Then she wriggled, thin sides bulging, into the den. Only two pups greeted her with a tiny form of the hunting salute. Whining, they jumped at Marta's face with wet snub noses. Their mother's breath had never smelled like this, and it excited them in ways they couldn't understand.

Meat drunk and still drowsy, Marta stumbled over Rann and Annie in her search for Sula. She found the little one lying in the back of the den. At Marta's approach, the pup's head came up. Sula was alive. When she wobbled to her feet, Marta felt her milk begin to flow, and for the first time since Calef's death, her heart felt its normal size. Marta sighed and dropped to her side. Sleep came instantly. She didn't even notice that it was Sula who found the first nipple.

After that night, Marta did not return to the ridge top.

a pack to call home

Raising the pups without Calef would not be easy, as Marta quickly learned. This was her first litter, and her first year as an alpha wolf; unlike Oldtooth, she did not have many seasons of experience feeding and leading a pack. But Marta had something else, something that showed in her hunting, her playing, her mothering— even, as time went by, in the angle of her ears and the cadence of her walk. That something was the instinct for survival.

Marta had a relentless will to live. It was an inner pulse that beat strong even when her body grew tired, a deep sinew that connected her to life. Without it, she would not have lived past puppyhood. Outcasts often die of starvation or attacks by other wolves—even members of their own pack—but Marta lived. She was fast enough to run from a fight, patient enough to wait for food, and smart enough to find danger before it found her.

Luck, too, was sometimes on her side. The role of outcast actually saved her back in the north. It was late winter, the hungriest season, in the second year of her life. Marta's pack was large and the snow was thin, so they had little advantage over the hooved deer and elk. When the wolves couldn't make a kill, they scavenged, digging up remains buried by lions or even, sometimes, stealing from coyotes.

One day they came upon an elk carcass unburied and uneaten, and the pack threw themselves upon it. As usual, Marta hung back, pacing in the cold. Now that she was fully grown, the friendly female no longer saved scraps or bones for her. Marta waited, pacing, as the ranking pack members carried away shanks and ribs, and even the young of the year, her brothers and sisters, gulped their share of meat.

Marta had stopped pacing and was eyeing her littlest brother, waiting for an opening, when her father began to retch. As always, he had eaten first and most, but this time he was not heaving meat for pups; his body was bucking and twisting so strangely that the rest of the pack, pups and all, stopped eating. Alarm swept through the group and they froze in place, steam rising from their reddened mouths. Within moments, their leader collapsed.

Marta backed away, her appetite gone. Her legs grew stiff and her belly tight as she watched her pack members, one by one, sicken and die. Some, like her mother, retched and collapsed violently as her father had. Others, like Marta's friend, grew feeble and staggered into the trees. A few—mainly the young of the year who had fed last and least—simply heaved up their meal and fell down, exhausted, in the snow. By nightfall only Marta and her younger brother were still alive. The rest of the pack had been poisoned.

Marta ran. Not knowing why or where, she ran. Leaving the dead and dying, leaving her brother, she ran until she could run no more. She ran for days that became weeks. She ran circles, spirals, and crazy-eights; diagonals, slashes, switchbacks, and zigzags. She ran from the danger, ran from the death, ran to survive.

As Marta ran, she learned. Where once she had learned from a distance, watching her elders, now she learned from the world around her. She learned to smell for traps and run detours around them. She learned to run with water and to run from strangers; she learned to run for food, killing large and small to stay alive. She learned to run from the scent of humans, and she never forgot the taint of poison. Pack or no pack, home or no home, Marta kept to one path: the path of survival.

It was in that time of running that she found Calef. Unlike other strange wolves, he proved friendly, and soon they were running together. With Calef, Marta learned to hunt as a team; together they could kill more, and more easily, than either could alone. For the first time in her life, with Calef Marta learned the pleasures of play. When it was time, they mated.

There in the north Marta and Calef had all they needed, except a home. Marta had left her birthplace far behind and now, wherever they ran they were the strangers, the outsiders. Where one wolf pack's territory ended, another's began. Where there were no wolves, there were bears or lions. Where there were no wolves or bears or lions, there was no food. Marta and Calef ran from valley to valley, looking for territory to make their own.

They traveled south. There, most of the valleys were filled with people. With people came cars and roads, bullets and traps; the smell of human beings was the smell of danger, and Calef and Marta ran out of their way to avoid it. It was on one such detour, a journey through the Kootenai Valley to the west, that they encountered Oldtooth. He too had come from the north. Between his age and his teeth, he was no threat to Calef and Marta, and they soon discovered that what he might lack in strength, he made up for in experience. The pack of two became three, and ran together.

They ran as far as Pleasant Valley, and there they stopped.

The valley had a long history. To run through it was to run through millions of years, from the rolling of the first seas to the wrinkling of the land that formed the Rocky Mountains. Some fifty million years ago the first ancestor of the wolf had walked here. For eons the land rose and fell under the paws and hooves of ancient creatures, building and eroding, flooding and reforming. Then for a time it lay silent under great sheets of ice: the animals disappeared, and Pleasant Valley took shape.

When the ice melted, there were no trees and no meadows—just a scoured landscape and a gentle gouge in the hills, half full of water. As rock turned to soil and hills turned to trees, the lake filled with rich sediment, forming the floor of the valley. A remnant of water, Dahl Lake, remained at the east end of the valley, and tall meadow grasses grew around it. By the time wildlife returned, the valley was perfect for deer—and perfect for wolf.

The wolves stopped and stayed. Pleasant Valley fit Marta like her own frosty-black coat. After only one season, she knew its creeks and ridges by heart. The pack had marked scent trails through forest and pasture, and she could find her way in fog, in rain, in a blizzard white as teeth or a night as black as Sula's soft, round head. Here, food was abundant. With or without Calef, this long dish of a valley would feed Marta better than her mother ever had.

Whether Marta could feed an ailing packmate and a litter of pups was another question. Oldtooth knew his arithmetic; what he didn't know was Marta. He didn't know her inner pulse. He did know that for an alpha wolf, the life of the pack was life itself.

Now, as the alpha of their pack, Marta's fierce will to live included them all. Her answer to wolf arithmetic was simple: three pups meant hunting three times as hard. She was no stranger to struggle. If there was one bone, she would gnaw it to the marrow; if there was one scrap, she would find it; if there was one way out of danger, she would chance it. Marta did not quit. The hard days of her youth became a strength that stayed with her.

With Pleasant Valley for a home, Marta for a pack leader, and any luck at all, the old wolf outside the den and the young ones in it—all of them—could live to see many seasons ahead.

SEVEN

monkey see, monkey do

As the days grew longer, so did Marta's hunts. In addition to milk, the pups were soon eating the meat she brought back in her belly and gave up for them at the den site. Nourished this way, the pups grew sturdy and round. They left the confines of the den and, under Oldtooth's supervision, explored the tiny forest world that lay within a few steps of their birthplace. They quickly discovered, as youngsters will, that everything was a toy: a stick, a pebble, a caterpillar, a moth, a scrap of hide, and sometimes—if they dared—Oldtooth himself.

The old wolf seemed to live for the little ones, though it wasn't always easy for him to keep up with them. He creaked from teeth to toes when he got up, but get up he did, and creak he did, the moment he heard the pups stirring. But his ears were not as keen as his nose, and sometimes the pups were on their second round of play by the time he finally wakened.

Oldtooth could not provide for the pack by killing big game, but he had an equally important role. While Marta was off hunting, he became the pups' guardian, teacher, disciplinarian, and gruff playmate. The youngsters were not allowed away from the den area, and if they lost track of the boundary—as sometimes happened—Oldtooth scolded them back. He had a terrifying growl, and the bite of his rounded teeth could leave a lasting impression on a wolf puppy's neck. Annie, the boldest of the three, had been returned to safety more than once in the clutch of their gray guardian's jaws.

Oldtooth showed complete patience with the pups, sometimes more than Marta. Rann already knew better than to try to pounce his mother awake. The one time he tried, it earned him a nip on the rear and an unforgettable gleam from a pair of huge yellow eyes.

Marta needed rest. Her sense of play had returned, but play came after work and these days, she had work to spare. Filling three small bellies was hard, especially when filling them only made the bellies larger and hungrier. Oldtooth continued to kill what he could, but once the pups reached their summer growth spurt, they were always hungry. Until late fall, when the young would be old enough to go along on hunts, their need for food would only grow. The more Calef's scent faded from the area, the more his pack needed him.

Though Calef's scent faded, his presence remained in the pups. Annie, the firstborn of the litter, was gray just like Calef, with the same black tip at the end of her tail and the same grace in her stride. Pouncing after grasshoppers, Annie was stronger and smoother than either Sula or Rann. Even in puppyhood, she was all power and precision: her father's kind of hunter.

If Annie was her father's hunter, Sula was her mother's daughter. Healthy now, growing as fast as her brother and sister, Sula was an echo of Marta's lean, frosted-black self. Sula was the one who would follow anyone anywhere, just to go along. But she was quickest to follow her mother, looking like a shadow of Marta as they trotted to the creek for a drink. Sula seemed happy just to be alive.

As for Rann—Rann was the clown of the litter. His head looked too big for his body, but then, his father had been enormous from head to tail. Big-boned, night-black, and born to tease, it was Rann who would stalk Oldtooth, napping in the sun. Creeping up on the old wolf, Rann would crouch—shoulders low and tail swishing—waiting for the right moment to pounce him awake. If Oldtooth was sleeping hard and the ambush failed, the little prankster tried not to look embarrassed as he circled around for a second try.

Rann was also the king of hide-and-seek. He never lost a game. In tall grass, behind tree stumps, around rocks, in or out of the den, he could always slink the lowest and hold still the longest. He barely seemed to breathe, or even blink. No matter how long Annie and Sula waited, he could wait longer—long enough, sometimes, for his sisters to get bored and find another game. When that happened, it wasn't long before Oldtooth would tip back his head, work his jaws, and start a long, soft coming-home howl. Annie and Sula would stop their playing, glance at Oldtooth, and lay back their heads in a pair of puppy howls. Before long Rann would appear, as if by magic. The sound of his pack was one thing that would bring him out from his hiding place.

When Marta was not hunting or sleeping, she was in the thick of the pack: feeding, teaching, protecting, and finally playing. The way of the wolf began at birth, and in the first months, it was learned through play. Every skill her babies would need to survive in the wild—running, tracking, attacking, keeping order, communicating—had its beginning in puppy games.

A favorite game was monkey see, monkey do, and it was played constantly at the wolf site. What the pups saw, they did. When Marta went to the creek for a drink, Sula followed. When Oldtooth pricked his ears at a smell, Annie pricked hers. When one pup found a stick to bite, the others had to have sticks too. When the adults howled a hunting song, the pups joined in. It was a game for the youngsters, but it formed the bonds of the pack; and as their elders knew, the way of the pack was the way of the wolf.

In tug-of-war the pups learned to keep their balance and how to look an opponent in the eye. They practiced the moves that would be used to tear hide from a carcass, building the muscles behind their jaws. In hide-and-seek, they learned to run from enemies and sneak up on prey. Who's in charge, a special wolf game, determined which pack members would make the best leaders and whose direction should be followed. Even hunting was still a game, as the pups pounced after dragonflies and stormed the nearby anthill.

The most important game, the pups quickly learned, was follow the leader. In the Pleasant Valley pack, everyone followed Marta. She was the alpha: she decided when to hunt and when to sleep, when the pups had to stay in the den and when it was time to leave. Oldtooth was next in line and took over when Marta was away. Even the pups had their own order. Since they were barely out of the den, Annie had been the leader of the three. So Sula and Rann followed Annie, and they all followed Oldtooth, who, in turn, followed Marta.

By the time the pups were two months old, their den site was littered with the happy debris of playthings. Bones and parts of bones, sticks and rocks, lichen and bark were strewn about the mouth of the den. Even a tuft of chewed plastic lay in the dirt, looking like dried gristle. The pups had not used the inner chamber for some time; Sula, who was now as tall as Annie, no longer crawled into it when she was frightened.

The young wolves were filling out, losing their scruffy, potbellied look and taking on a long-boned leanness. The leggier they got, the more restless they grew. Once they knew every stick and pebble around the den, they started to stray toward the woods when no one was watching. If they didn't come running, tails tucked, at Oldtooth's growl, worse was in store; the pups were still not too big to be grabbed by the scruff of the neck and hauled unceremoniously home.

One drizzly morning, the youngsters were at their usual business. Rann was digging frantically for buried treasure. Annie was digging along with him, until a butterfly caught her eye. She chased the butterfly around and around until she spied Sula chewing on a piece of bark. When Sula stopped to shake the crumbs off her tongue, Annie snatched up the bark and pranced away, carrying it proudly toward the woods and watching Sula's reaction from the corner of her eye. Sula hesitated, then picked up another piece of bark and continued chewing, watching Annie.

Rann abruptly stopped digging. He and Sula followed with their eyes as Annie paraded toward the trees with her loot. Where was she going? Rann turned to catch up with her, and the game of monkey see, monkey do was on. Annie sniffed at a stump. Rann sniffed at the stump. She squatted and marked. He squatted and marked. Sula dropped her bark and scrambled to join them, and together they sniffed and marked their way deeper and deeper into the woods.

Monkey see, monkey do became follow the leader, with Annie in charge. The farther they went, the more complicated she made it, and soon they had left the safe zone of the den. So intent were they on discovering and following that they did not hear Oldtooth's warning sound. Annie kept leading, and Rann and Sula kept following; there were tracks they'd never smelled, grasses they'd never tasted, and scurrying sounds they'd never heard.

Suddenly a tremendous commotion erupted in front of them. Something gray and black and snarling, an eight-legged monster, appeared in their path. The thing snapped and growled at them, a writhing mass of fur and many, many teeth. The pups cringed together, making themselves as small as possible—and abruptly, the snarling stopped. The legs sorted out into two sets of four, one black and one gray. The teeth disappeared behind two familiar faces: Marta and Oldtooth. The pups had never seen such stern looks, and they flattened their chests to the ground, slicking back their ears and looking up at their elders. Even Annie, bravest of the three, stretched back her lips in an apologetic grin and thumped her tail on the ground.

The pups cowered, waiting for a gruff bark to send them back to the den or for the feel of teeth lifting them by the neck. Neither came. Instead, Marta turned and marched off in the opposite direction, away from the den. The pups half rose and hesitated, whining and looking at Oldtooth. He barked then, a sharp command directed at Marta's disappearing backside, and the pups shot off after their mother. It was time to see the world.

EIGHT

rendezvous

It was raining hard by the time Marta led her pack down the draw. The pups' bravado was gone, and as they left their home behind, their eyes grew wide and their gait nervous. Sula walked stiff-legged, as if each foot was on fire, and Rann and Annie huddled close, bumping sides as they hurried along behind their mother. Oldtooth brought up the rear, nose keen for dangers. The wolves followed the creek from which they drank, winding downstream through fir and pine trees toward the great expanse of Pleasant Valley.

Not far from the den, the path became a grassy road and the stream became a pond with a small dam at one end. Beyond the dam, encircled by the dirt road, lay Dahl Lake and the long meadows of Pleasant Valley. The pups had never seen so much sky. At the edge of the trees, the gray June ceiling rolled out and out in front of them. By now Sula's feet were barely touching the ground, and Rann and Annie seemed connected by magnetic force. Marta and Oldtooth halted at the road, listening, then shot across the road and into the meadow.

The pups followed close behind, and the moment their feet hit the long, wet grasses on the other side, something happened. Marta and Oldtooth bounded into the meadow without a backward glance and the pups, following their leaders, did the same. Stretching their legs for the first time in a true wolf run, they were unstoppable. All fear disappeared in that instant, and it was playtime again—playtime like they had never known.

Dahl Lake was more water than a pack could ever drink. With a yip, Annie bounced gleefully toward it, Rann still close at her side. Sula outdid them both; she was taking a fast lap around the shore by the time they reached the water's edge. While the pups raced toward the lake, Marta and Oldtooth made up their own game of high-speed tag, hide-and-seek, and leapfrog. Blinking against the rain, Marta raced toward the glade of aspen trees with Oldtooth in pursuit. Halfway to the trees she stopped flat, dropped into the soaked grass, and let Oldtooth soar over her in a low-flying bound. No sooner had his front feet hit the ground than she was up and galloping after him again. Then Oldtooth dropped, Marta leaped, and places changed again.

The black cattle grazing in the meadow had seen Marta and Oldtooth many times, passing through on their hunts, and barely glanced at the revelry going on around the aspens and the lake. A few cows moved mildly down valley to give the pups—especially Sula, who had found her stride—room to run.

The cattle's movement caught Oldtooth's eye, and for a moment he gave chase to a cow instead of Marta. He wasn't hungry—Marta had brought down a deer just days before—and the animal seemed to know it wasn't a real chase. The cow ran a few steps, then lumbered away with a grunt. Oldtooth followed at an easy distance, sniffing idly at the tracks and leaving Marta to explore the aspen trees.

When Marta found nothing of interest in the trees, she howled for her pack. The pups had never heard the come-here call from such a distance and came thrashing through the meadow, tongues flapping and coats soaked with rain. When Oldtooth arrived, the pack joined together in a long and happy song, then followed as Marta led them back to the road.

At the dam, instead of turning toward the den, she continued along the road before heading up a different draw. In a small clearing there, as the pups would soon find, were the remains of a whitetail Marta had killed. She had carried some of its meat back to the den in her belly, and its flavor was strong. As they approached, Annie picked up the smell and whined, wrinkling her brow and looking from her mother to Oldtooth. Marta quickened her pace, and soon they were in the clearing.

At the wolves' approach, ravens that had been picking at the carcass flapped into the trees and began a loud argument. The pups scattered at the wing beats, ducking behind Oldtooth, and peeked at the dead deer with great interest. They craned their necks, but held back with their feet, waiting to be shown what to do. Marta sniffed a circle around the kill site, alert for traps and poison. Next she approached the carcass itself, examining each section as gingerly as if it could bite. Satisfied, Marta tore into the deer's shoulder, yanking back the hide with a practiced move the pups knew from tug-of-war.

Annie got the idea immediately. As if she'd done it all her life, she reached forward and bit into the muscle her mother had exposed. But Annie's milk teeth, though sharp, were no match for the flesh of the deer, and after much pulling and growling, she came up with only a small mouthful of shreds. These she carried off proudly and swallowed with a gulp. Before she could run back for another mouthful, monkey see became monkey do, and Rann and Sula were in her way. As Annie barged between them, Marta continued pulling hide from the rump. Oldtooth, with his blunted teeth, waited like the pups for flesh to be exposed; when there was room, he reached in with a grunt and clamped his jaws around a mouthful of the good, strong meat.

While the pups and Oldtooth did what they could with the teeth they had, Marta used her canines and incisors to strip the carcass. When the deer was skinned, she twisted off a foreleg and dragged it under the raven tree. She gnawed peacefully on the bone, watching her youngsters relish their first fresh meal.

The rain let up, turning to mist as they ate, and the pups began to complain. Their pulling and tugging and tearing was not filling their bellies, so Marta left her leg bone to break off single ribs, dropping one each for the pups. They fought for the meatiest rib, Annie nosing out Rann, and Sula getting the last pick. Then Marta broke off a few more ribs and left them in reach of Oldtooth. The pack feasted until the gray sky grew steely and dark—but Marta did not rise again to lead them back to their old home. This would be their home for now, the first of the summer rendezvous sites where the pack would meet and eat and rest. They would not return to the den again.

NINE

growing pains

Although the pups no longer needed the den, moving away from it was a heady adventure. In a single afternoon they went from a safe world they knew, down to the last blade of grass, to a completely new world—full of things to explore, but full of uncertainties too. The pups saw by the cautious way Marta and Oldtooth moved that they, too, had to be watchful here. The days of puppyhood, however short, were already over.

The rendezvous site was a halfway place between the safety of the den and the freedom of the forest. As the pups grew, Marta and Oldtooth would let their world grow with them. A clearing like this gave the young wolves more room to play and explore while keeping them safe from the full-size dangers of the forest. Only when they were big enough to survive on their own would they be given full freedom to roam.

The pack stayed at their first rendezvous site for several weeks. Within days the deer carcass was picked clean, and Annie made an endless game of the bones. She teased Sula with the forelegs and played soccer with the skull. Sula, since she had discovered running, wanted nothing else to do; she wore a path around the clearing in ever-faster circles. Once again Rann was champion of hide-and-seek, camouflaging himself among the stumps and shadows in the clearing. The pups sharpened their hunting skills, graduating from grasshoppers to mice, and chasing any hapless rabbits that came too close.

With the deer carcass reduced to bones, it was time for Marta to hunt again. She called the pack together for a howl, and the voices that drifted into the sky were longer and throatier than before; the pups were growing up. After a wet salute from her pack, Marta loped away. In a matter of moments Annie had dragged off the pelvic bone from the deer, and Rann and Sula were playing hide-and-seek. Sula's idea of "seeking" was to race around the clearing at top speed, so Rann was hidden for longer than usual. The pups thus occupied, Oldtooth trotted out to sniff the breeze for squirrels. Now that the youngsters needed less supervision, he could leave long enough to hunt a small meal.

Sula ran around and around the rendezvous site, but when Rann still did not come out, she grew bored. Finding him in none of the usual hiding spots, she ran to join Annie's attack on the hipbone. It was a fine toy, big enough for two, complete with shreds of meat to fight over. The game had turned to full scale tug-of-war—Sula losing—when they heard a terrified howl from beyond the clearing. Annie dropped her end of the bone, and Sula fell backward in surprise.

The yowl was followed by thrashing and barking—Rann's voice!—from a nearby thicket. A terrifying medley of sounds made Sula and Annie dive for cover under the nearest bush. A fearsome fight was taking place, and when their brother's bark turned to a distressed squeal, Annie sprang out of the shrubs and dashed toward the sound.

Halfway across the clearing, she was cut off by Oldtooth. He looked huge, standing sideways with his gray ruff raised around glittering eyes. Annie stopped in her tracks. Sula peeked out from behind her bush, but when Oldtooth flicked an ear her way, she popped back in. The noise in the thicket tripled, and in the bedlam they heard a new sound. It was their mother—and yet it was not. It was Marta's voice, but none of the pups had ever heard such a shriek; her fiercest scolding was gentle by comparison. This was the voice of teeth, the promise of death.

That promise made, suddenly there came a screech from the brush, and a tawny shape shot across the clearing behind Oldtooth. No taller than Annie, the bobcat was fat and fast, and it streaked out of sight before Oldtooth could manage a hoarse bark. Annie crouched motionless, and Sula stayed hidden until the noise died away. Oldtooth, having caught his breath, finally galloped after the tail-less end of the cat.

In a few moments Marta appeared from the thicket, carrying Rann by the neck as she had when the pups were infants. His whole body drooped, from the ears to the nose and from his shoulders down to his slack tail. The coal-black fur was matted with spittle and spiked with blood.

Sula crept out from hiding and tiptoed toward Annie, who slowly rose from her crouch. Stock-still, they watched Marta lay the black shape in the grass under a young fir. The legs and hindquarters were limp, but as soon as his shoulder touched the ground, Rann exploded with a wail. He was alive. Though bleeding from many scratches and from a paw-size slash on his shoulder, Rann gave a cry that was the sound of life, not death. Marta cleaned the wounds, tugging loose skin back where it belonged with her fine front teeth. She treated Rann from nose to tail, smoothing his roughed coat with strong strokes of her tongue.

Except for his shoulder, Rann was in one piece. When the bleeding finally slowed and Marta paused in her treatment, Annie and Sula whimpered. Rann stirred, as if to get up and play, but something stopped him: a long, low growl from the black throat of his mother. She shaped her form around his in a protective half-circle, and slowly the warning growl turned to a contented grumble. Survived again.

TEN

oldtooth's find

After Rann's misadventure, Marta put off her hunt. She tended his wounds constantly, sniffing each puncture and sometimes cleaning so deeply that Rann yelped in pain. While Marta stayed close, keeping him from the temptation to play, Oldtooth returned to the woods in search of small game. Annie and Sula became adept mouse hunters who gobbled down their catch instead of offering, as Oldtooth did, to share. But the squirrels and rabbits Oldtooth brought back were not filling their bellies, and the deer carcass in the clearing was still a litter of blood-marked bones.

By the time Rann's shoulder had closed, the whole pack was out of sorts from hunger. One afternoon Oldtooth returned to the rendezvous site with his ears high and his tail waving like a young willow. Rounding his lips and lifting his chin, he howled an unexpected song: the feasting song. Marta cocked her head, hesitating; Oldtooth always carried small kills back in his mouth. This song meant there was something he couldn't carry.

Marta studied Oldtooth, who continued to howl until she, too, raised her head and sang. Then the pups ran to greet their old friend and join in the howl. They licked and nipped at Oldtooth's muzzle, but Marta did not do the same; she was the alpha wolf, regardless of who did the hunting. Still, it was Oldtooth who led the pack away from the clearing, slowed only by Rann's limp, out toward the big meadow and the lake.

As soon as Sula saw the fringe of treetops give way to the Pleasant Valley sky, she began to zig and zag from their single-file formation, but she knew better than to bolt before Marta gave the sign. At the road they heard grunts from range cattle and the drone of a tractor in the distance. As Marta and Oldtooth flicked their ears and sniffed the air, the pups sniffed and listened too.

Finally Oldtooth led them across the meadow, past the grazing cattle. Marta's nose twitched at their smell, but the wave in Oldtooth's tail promised food—and they all needed food.

At the edge of the meadow, where the land buckled into a pine-dotted hillside, the smell of death hit Marta's nostrils. It was not the smell of a wolf kill; there was no salty tang of blood, no sign of a chase or struggle, no flesh or hide strewn about. Oldtooth led on, and when they saw the size of his quarry, it was obvious why he had not carried it back. But this was no deer: it was a steer. A black yearling lay in the lengthening sun, its head buzzing with flies.

The animal had died on its own, with no help from Oldtooth, and the wolves were not the first to find it. Where the belly was chewed open, the smell of coyote was strong. Marta approached tentatively, ears forward, instincts troubled. Since the poisoning of her pack in the north, she rarely ate anything she didn't kill. Though cattle weren't her choice of food, their meat could become tolerable—if not tantalizing—when she was hungry enough. After nearly a week since her last meal, she was almost that hungry.

Marta was not that hungry, but her pack was. The pups, who had developed an appetite for meat, whined at the smell. Sensing nothing unnatural, Marta bit once at the opening in the steer's belly. Then, fighting back the odors of cow and coyote, she jerked angrily at the skin, which was tougher than deer hide—almost as thick as moose. The pups hung back as she worked, sniffing curiously at the strange-smelling meat. When they saw Marta opening the carcass like a deer, they surged around her to get at the food. Oldtooth had to steady the body, holding a leg in his jaws, while Marta pulled away the skin. Meanwhile, the pups gobbled up the smaller organs they could swallow without much chewing.

Marta kept skinning. She worked grimly, fur flat and eyes narrowed. Hungry though they were, the pups mimicked their mother's mood; her tail did not wag, and neither did theirs. Finally she stopped to circle the steer, sniffing at each of the pups and inspecting Rann's shoulder. His skin was holding. Now Marta stopped to gulp some scraps for herself, but she had to swallow hard to get them down. This was not good food. Wrinkles appeared in Marta's black brow as she watched her pack grow red-mouthed around the body of the steer.

ELEVEN

first warning

One evening in midsummer, having left the pups with Oldtooth at their latest rendezvous site, Marta killed a young elk in the aspen grove by the lake. Rann's injury had healed, and she was back to hunting as before. Crossing the road toward the rendezvous, a happy howl rising, the sound suddenly caught in her throat. Something was wrong.

The dusty road had been traveled since she crossed it, and there were human footprints on the path next to the dam. Marta's hair prickled on her back as she sniffed out the tracks. One set seemed to amble without direction, but the other went past the pond and up the stream, straight toward the old den site. Fighting the urge to run, Marta followed the tracks, her breathing short. Darkness gathered in the trees, and soon she was moving on scent alone. Her gait grew cautious as she edged along the creek, stopping now and then to listen, to smell the air or to bury her nose in a moist footprint. There were no sounds, and no trace of human breath in the cooling air. Marta continued.

She was almost to the den when a new smell assaulted her nose. Her body went rigid, as if to disappear into the shadows. This was not a smell she had found in Pleasant Valley: it was the scent of a strange wolf, a trespasser. Marta's hackles went up, and the fur swelled around her neck. A low growl, almost inaudible, rumbled through her throat.

The first strange wolf Marta met nearly killed her. It happened in the north, shortly after her pack died. She was in her first breeding period, a time that turned her instincts upside down. Marta had been traveling for miles without a real meal when she heard a convention of ravens on a hillside. She followed her stomach toward the noise.

She never got there. Posted around the kill site, on stumps and rocks and patches of snow, was the scent mark of a strange wolf, a sign that said KEEP OUT. Marta had seen her father and mother lead the pack away from such smells, and she bared her teeth at it. She sniffed again, trying to guess how long ago the sign had been posted and how far away its owner was, when suddenly a growl came from behind.

It was a black wolf. Marta was too young, too confused, and too hungry to fight, so she simply fled. The strange wolf chased her for miles, in and out of the creek, up and down the hillsides. Marta was faster, but he knew the terrain better, and finally he cornered her against a short cliff.

But he did not attack. He did not snarl or threaten. Instead, he began sniffing aggressively at her and whining as if he were hurt. As she cowered, ears flat, suddenly he reared up and placed his paws on her shoulders, something that hadn't happened since she was a scruff-ball pup. Marta backed against the rock wall and before she could shake him off, something in her snapped. The smell and the strangeness and the hunger exploded together, and she spun out from under him like a leaf in whitewater.

Fangs bared, she went for the wolf's leg. When she felt a bone crush between her jaws, the blood madness boiled up and she clung fast to his foreleg. He snarled, but in the instant before he lunged, she released her bite and ran. Sickened by the taste of wolf blood, she ran harder and harder until she heaved the taste from her mouth. She never saw or smelled that black wolf's sign again, and from that day, Marta regarded strangers as enemies until they proved otherwise.

Today in Pleasant Valley, the strange wolf scent was mixed with the scent of humans, and as Marta was sorting out the two signals, she picked up a third: the high-pitched smell of metal. Metal on or under the ground, not far from her feet. This was no strange wolf. It was a trap.

Cautiously, she strained her nose toward the metal. It was set right where she would have turned from the creek toward the den. She knew to avoid these smells, but the pups did not. As their range grew, this was one of the first places they would come to explore.

Marta backed away. But instead of turning and running down the path, she did something she had seen Oldtooth do once after she and Calef met him in the Kootenai. She picked her way down the shallow bank of the creek and pawed through the stream bed. The creek was only a trickle at this time of year, and she didn't have to hunt long for what she wanted. Marta dug furiously, spattering herself with mud, until she unearthed a large rock. It was nearly the size of Rann's head, and though her jaws fit easily around it, the weight strained her neck as she hoisted herself over the bank and back onto the trail.

There she dropped the stone with a thud, shook the muck from her coat, and sniffed past the twigs and leaves for the wolf-metal-human scent. The whole area reeked, and it made Marta's nose ache. She picked up the stone again and took a step toward the source of the smell. Lifting the rock as high as she could, neck trembling, she turned her head to the side and opened her jaws. The stone broke through the twigs, bounced off one side of the trap, and onto the trip plate. The metal jaws sprang closed with a dull clank.

Marta jumped at the sound she had made. The forest was silent now, engulfed in blackness. She sniffed around the sprung trap and its drag chain, marked the metal fiercely with her own scent, then turned and made her way up the trail toward the den. The human footprints looped crazily, wandering from side to side across the draw, but eventually they, too, reached the mouth of the den. It was ripe with human scent; Marta could almost feel the skin of fingers exploring the clay walls. She shook. That scent would fade, and for now she had no need of the den.

Marta continued up the draw, taking a shortcut over to the rendezvous site. Though the human sign stopped at the den, she jumped at every sound, and her nose swung sharply to the tang of any new scent. It was not until she reached the clearing, receiving the hungry whines and licks from her pack, that the feasting howl finally came loose from her throat. There was still a meal of elk waiting for them in the aspen grove.

TWELVE

meadow days

After the trap appeared, Marta moved the pack's rendezvous site to the aspen grove at Dahl Lake. The island of trees could be seen from the road, but from it, intruders on the road could also be watched in safety. In the meadow the pups had more room to run and play, and the stately aspens gave shelter from traffic on the road or in the air. The pack quickly finished the elk—these days, each pup was eating almost as much as Oldtooth—and Marta expanded her hunting routes.

More and more often in her travels, she came upon the sign of humans. She found grasses freshly flattened and shrubs brushed aside by something other than the narrow legs of elk and deer. She found footprints at their old rendezvous sites and bones missing or moved from kills. She smelled the scents of the same individuals whose footprints had led to the trap. Quiet Pleasant Valley, with its wide margin between wolves and humans, was not so quiet anymore.

It was almost time to start taking the young wolves out to hunt, but for now, Marta was keeping the pack close together at the aspens. Oldtooth returned to clean up the remains of the steer he had discovered, but coyotes had done their work, and there was nothing left but hide and bones. Always looking for an easy meal, he found another dead cow—a scrawny one that had starved to death—and for a few days took one or another of the pups on midnight raids to scavenge the meat. Marta concentrated on wild game, afterward leading the pack to the kill sites but always returning to the aspens. She neither prevented nor went along with the nighttime raids. The pups' heads now came almost to her shoulders, and she had stopped nursing entirely. To keep growing, they required more meat than she alone could provide.

The days grew shorter. Sunrise came later over the eastern hills, and sunset earlier from the west. Afternoon skies reddened with the haze of forest fires, and mornings started crisp and dry. Signs of humans continued to appear, but Marta found no more traps.

Summer ripened over the great meadow of Pleasant Valley. While Annie hunted rabbits—she had graduated from mice—Sula ran and ran. She chased anything for fun, even a calf, if one was nearby. She would chase her own shadow if she could find nothing else. Rann, meanwhile, perfected his hiding skills. He hid in the aspen grove and practiced standing still in the grasses that waved over his head. Marta and Oldtooth were hunting much of the time, but they sometimes played and sometimes rested, watching the youngsters grow and explore.

Road traffic increased, and the pack played hide-and-seek from the cars that drove and sometimes stopped on the road near the dam. Except for the increased traffic, the wolves were not disturbed.

On these late summer days, Marta wakened early and surveyed her sleeping pack. The pups had grown lanky and long. With weeks of good eating and good exercise, they had nearly doubled in weight. Sula and Annie were the same size now. Rann, the largest, seemed to be catching up in size with his father's massive skull. All their coats had grown in thick, and the three sleeping shapes—two black and one gray—bore little resemblance to the round, wet creatures she had birthed back in the den. Even Oldtooth was keeping a certain plumpness under his tattered coat, though Marta didn't always know what he was eating.

So far, Marta's genius for survival had held the pack together. Despite Oldtooth's fearful arithmetic, despite hunger and attack and now intrusions, all the pups had lived. The pack was whole and healthy. As soon as the youngsters got a little bigger and their real teeth came in, they would join Marta and Oldtooth as part of the hunting team. With five hunters and no small mouths to feed, they would face winter well prepared.

But then more traps appeared.

THIRTEEN

kidnapped

Sula and Annie stepped into traps on the same afternoon. It was a late day in summer, raining again. Coming back from a carcass Oldtooth had found at the edge of the meadow, Annie noticed a strange smell: wolf smell, but not one of their pack. More curious than afraid, she went to investigate, and Rann and Sula followed.

The pups had not received Marta's lesson on avoiding human smells and metal smells—especially when they appeared together—and Marta was not there. She was tracking a deer, trying as ever to keep up with her pack's mountainous appetite. As for Oldtooth, he had lagged behind the youngsters and trouble was upon them before he knew it.

First Annie and then Sula were caught by surprise.

As one trap snapped around Annie's foreleg, she burst into an almighty cry. Sula, backing away, caught her back leg in a different trap. Helpless at their howls, Old-tooth and Rann sprinted for the aspens. On the ridge, Marta stopped her hunt in midstep. She turned her head slowly toward the meadow, ears trembling with the shrill sounds rising into the heavy overcast. She stood for a moment, then turned and raced toward the cries of her young.

Before she could reach the road, a vehicle drove up slowly and stopped near the traps. Someone got out. The wolves' wails were suddenly silent. Another vehicle arrived. Unseeing, listening only for clues from the meadow, Marta walked past a grazing deer as she skulked down from the ridge. Seeing the vehicles, she kept out of sight, a shadow that paced the fringe of trees on the far side of the road.

Marta could not see Annie and Sula. She could only see people and trucks and ropes and guns. The activity was quiet, almost gentle; once the pups stopped howling, there were no loud noises. A human figure approached the aspens, but before it got near, Rann and Oldtooth darted out the other side, disappearing into the deep meadow. The grasses waved wetly here and there, as if wolves were lurking everywhere—or nowhere.

After a time, the people and vehicles left as quietly as they came. Sula and Annie were nowhere to be found.

Dusk came, a gray, wet dusk, and Marta shook the rain from her coat. The valley was silent: no calls from her daughters. No bluebird songs. Just the sound of water dripping from leaves. Marta stood and filled her lungs. The cry started in her belly, growing as it circled through her chest and out the bellows of her throat. The howl rose and fell, rose and fell across the bowl of Pleasant Valley. When she was done, there was a long silence. Darkness settled. And in the silence, first one, then two songs rose to her ears from near the aspens: Oldtooth and Rann. We are alive. We are here.

Then silence. Then silence.

FOURTEEN

trap smart

Annie and Sula were not gone long. In a few days vehicles arrived again. People got out and busied themselves, and left in their vehicles. When they were gone, two cages stood side by side near the aspens. In one was Annie and in the other, Sula.

Marta waited until night. When all was dark and there was no traffic and no sign of movement near the meadow, she approached. One footfall after another brought her near and she whined softly, a long breath with an edge. Hearing her, Annie and Sula hurled themselves against the wire and plastic, howling in a way that was no longer puppy-like. Marta's heart thumped against her chest as she prowled toward the cages, nose to the ground and then to the air, inspecting each blade of grass as if it could reach up and snap at her.

Two lengths from the kennels, she balked. A ridge of hair rose along her spine, and she opened her lips in a menacing grin. A threat clattered from her throat, so loud and so convincing that Annie and Sula quit howling and cowered in their crates. Then Marta barked sharply, a command that pulled Rann and Oldtooth from the aspens. As they ventured forward, she mixed threat and command, command and threat; Rann and Oldtooth moved uncertainly toward her.

The threats were not directed at Marta's packmates but at a point on the ground directly in front of her. A strong smell of strange wolf urine rose from that point, halfway between the free wolves and the caged. The smell was mixed with the scent of metal and the scent of humans: another trap.

With no stones nearby, Marta could not spring this trap. Instead she called Rann closer, caution rattling in her throat, and taught him a lesson not to forget. She watched as he sniffed the strange mix of scent, and as soon as his nose came too close to the trap, she snarled. If he drew back, she stopped snarling. If he did anything else, she snapped hard, teeth closing next to the delicate skin around his nose. He sniffed again, more cautiously: another snarl. Too close: another snap. Only a few lessons were needed before the smell of the trap—the mixture of metal, human, and strange wolf—connected with the snap of his mother's smooth teeth on his whiskers. Rann backed away from the smell.

Marta continued moving toward the kennels, sniffing at each step, and Rann and Oldtooth followed. No more traps appeared. When she was close enough, Marta charged Sula's cage. The kennel rocked under her, sending the frightened pup sliding into her trays of food and water. Annie attacked the metal grating on her door, but her teeth only plucked a dull tune on the wire. Marta threw herself at Annie's kennel then, but it too was well anchored. She alternately growled and bit at the cages, and licked and sniffed at the captives inside, but could not get through. Oldtooth and Rann howled plaintively, sending Annie and Sula into a frenzy.

After a time Rann and Oldtooth slinked back into the aspens, but Marta stayed on. She divided her time between licking her pups and attacking their enclosures. She chewed at the wires until her mouth grew sore and she tasted blood. Only when a tooth grew loose—one of her grappling canines—did she stop.

Exhausted, she lay down by the kennels. The pups finally slept, and Marta stayed until the sky grew light. She rose then, and retreated to the aspen rendezvous. All day she hid; at night, she traveled back toward the pups, skirting the traps that lay in her path. Every few days, people came to bring food and water for the pups and to clean their cages. Annie and Sula were by turns anxious and listless. Their coats grew dull. Their packmates remained hidden, watching the watchers who came and went from their valley. Traffic came and went on the road, and the sky seemed alive with huge metal birds. Every day a helicopter or airplane buzzed the hills and meadows where the wolves were hiding.

Oldtooth wandered the meadow, scavenging and hunting in his old way. Rann followed Oldtooth or Marta—the three rarely moved together now—and sometimes went off on his own. Though alive, the pack was in tatters. Singing, hunting, grooming, playing, and teaching were things of the past; only survival mattered. All that was natural, ordinary, and instinctive faded like the long days of summer.

Oldtooth was trapped next. Coming from one of his scavenger hunts, distracted by calls from Annie and Sula, Oldtooth stepped into a trap near the aspen grove. He was taken away but, unlike the pups, did not return.

That left Marta and Rann, and sometimes Annie and Sula. The noise overhead grew more constant. Under the roar of the blades, Marta crouched in the trees or streaked through the long meadow grasses. Sometimes, Rann was a dark ripple parting the green behind her.

As days passed, the urge to run, to run farther and longer than she had ever run before, grew strong, but

Rann was too young to travel far, and Annie and Sula could not run at all. Marta's survival instinct worked overtime. She bit at the cages at night and hid from traffic during the day; early or late, she hunted to feed Rann. Together they dodged the traps.

She did not even notice when the tranquilizer dart hit. She had left the tall grass, racing across the flat and up the hillside, and under the thundering helicopter, the sting of the dart blended with the beat of the wind and the thrashing of the long grass blades. Then all was dim, dimmer, dark.

FIFTEEN

reunited

When Marta awakened, the world was gone. Swirling around her was a cave of spinning lights with shifting sides, and she could not tell which way was up or down—if up or down existed anymore. Sounds came out of nowhere and then disappeared into nowhere, as in a dream. Marta whined, and her own voice came back in waves, sour and twisted, to her ears.

Gradually the lights and sounds steadied around her. When she could see and hear clearly, the world as she knew it was indeed gone. Pleasant Valley had disappeared. There was no grass, no soil, no trees, no sky. She was in a big, square den: a box with a flat stone bottom covered with straw and sides made of stone and wire. There was a tightness around her neck, a stout band of some kind, and the smell of humans was overpowering.

The smell of metal, and other smells she did not know, filled her head.

But she was not alone. There on the other side of the wire, out of their small kennels and placed in a large cage like her own, were Annie and Sula. Whining eagerly, the two pups poked their noses through the wire grid, trying to wiggle through the links to reach their mother. Marta rose to go to them, but dizziness set in. When the room stopped spinning she saw that there, on the far side of the pups, was Oldtooth. He turned to her, but did not rise. He gave no sign, not even the flop of his tail, and seemed to look through rather than at her. Marta sniffed nervously, whined once to the pups, then sank back down to the cold floor.

As for Rann—Rann was nowhere to be seen. The champion of hide-and-seek had gotten away.

PART TWO

SIXTEEN

the bad dream

The sound of voices forced Marta from her daze. Two steps away, just the other side of the wire grid, was a group of people staring at her. From their mouths came a flat music, more of a drone than a howl, and her head reeled with their smell—so many, and so close! Marta pressed herself into the straw. Ears slicked back and eyes downcast, she felt a tremor run through her legs. The urge to run was unbearable. But the people made no motion to come closer, and the murmurs ceased as a louder, deeper voice took over.

A brilliant flash struck the room, and Marta winced. There was no thunder, just a sharp *click* followed immediately by another flash. Marta winced again and turned toward the wall, legs trembling. The voice droned on.

A door banged open, and a wave of fresh air swept

through the place. A young woman in a white lab coat joined the group at the cages. Her smell, drifting toward Marta, was somehow familiar, as if the two had recently touched. She began to speak, and the other voice stopped. Her sound was soft and did not grate on the wolf's ears. The woman nodded at Marta and gestured toward Oldtooth, then stopped talking. The deeper voice resumed.

From the corner of her eye, Marta could see Oldtooth lying still in his cage. Like Marta and the pups, he also wore a thick collar with a small box that hung under his chin. For once, his big gray face held no expression at all: not the hunting face, the play face, or the warning face. It was hardly a face at all, despite the familiar arrangement of features. His eyes stared into the distance. His left foot was wrapped in white and stretched out straight in front of him.

The people moved on to Annie and Sula's cage. At this the pups glanced uneasily in Marta's direction, then Oldtooth's, but the adults gave no sign. When people touched their fingers to the wire, the pups cowered in the corner. Sula whined at the smell, and the room again spun around Marta. Her claws gripped the floor as if it were tilting. When she regained her balance, she could hear the deeper voice again, moving past Oldtooth's cage. The people were out of sight now, and her trembling eased.

The voices faded, and the wolves were left alone in their bright, flat surroundings. Human scent thickened the air. On the other side of the door a dog barked, jerking the wolves to attention. Marta growled, as if by reflex.

Nothing in Marta's life had prepared her for this: not the harsh days in the north or the death of her pack, not her life alone or her travels with Calef and Oldtooth. Her survival had always depended on her surroundings, but these surroundings were different. Her instincts were useless. Her first instinct, to run, was checked by the walls of stone and metal around her. She couldn't leap them without a running start, and the cage left no room for that. Her second instinct was to dig, and that proved futile too. After the people left, Marta pawed through the bed of straw, but all she found was a solid concrete floor. She had no urge to follow her third instinct, chewing: her mouth was still sore from trying to free Annie and Sula from their kennels at the aspen grove.

Marta's teeth and feet were useless here, and her great nose was crowded with scents so strange that she could not tell one from the other. Without teeth and feet and nose, her mind could not work. Her heart still pumped and her eyes and ears still gathered information, but she could do nothing with it. The deciding, reacting part of her shut down. When she was hungry, she picked at the deer meat that appeared in her cage. When she was thirsty, she lapped vaguely at the water in her bowl. Her fierce will to live was nowhere to be seen.

Days came and went. Groups of people came and went as well, always talking, often with the flashes and clicks that made Marta wince. A tarp was hung over the wire, and fewer eyes peered into the wolves' cages, but sometimes little people came and pressed their faces close, or even wiggled small fists through the wire until a big hand came and pulled them back. Whenever people approached, Marta grew edgy. Though her legs ached to run, she did not even stand. When the people left and her shaking quieted, she lay motionless in the straw. She stared, or slept.

A cage away, Oldtooth also stared and slept. In between, Annie and Sula ate little. They played halfheartedly with each other and with bones from the meat they were fed. They could not curb their curiosity about the people who came and went, and sometimes sniffed at the fingers pressed through the wires. Sometimes they slept, and sometimes whined to their elders. But the only example Marta and Oldtooth offered was stillness, and the pups were too young to practice stillness.

After a few days, the stream of visitors ended suddenly.

Marta came to recognize the woman in the white lab coat who, along with another young woman, was the only one who passed through the hallway now. They brought the wolves food and water and spread clean straw over the concrete. The woman in white paused sometimes at Oldtooth's cage, and bent down to look at the dressing on his paw. She let Annie and Sula lick her fingers through the cage, and though she moved gently, she still made Marta tremble and turn her head.

As time passed, Marta sorted through the confusion of smells. Most of the scent was human, so strong and fresh that it overwhelmed all others. But there were animal smells too: some old, some new, almost none of them wild. The scent of domestic dog was strong and made her cage seem very, very small.

One day, Marta watched as a small group of people joined the woman in white outside Oldtooth's cage. She gestured to his injured paw and spoke. A man with a long, slender stick slid it through the wire mesh and poked Oldtooth neatly in the rear. The wolf jumped in surprise, then relaxed. The man pulled the stick away. The people waited as the tranquilizer took effect, then cautiously entered Oldtooth's cage. A man held Oldtooth's head in his lap as the woman bent over his paw, cleaning it with a strong-smelling solution and dressing it again with a fresh bandage. The people spoke in low voices as she worked. They lay Oldtooth back on the straw, stepped out, and closed the cage door.

Then the people came to Marta's cage, and before she knew what was happening, she felt a sharp poke in her own backside. Then the world dimmed again, as it had once before. Vaguely, Marta felt a tightening around her muzzle, then around her front feet, then her back feet. Then darkness.

When Marta awoke, her feet were bound front and back, and her jaws were tied shut with a rope. The golden straw and smooth block walls whirled around her as she struggled against the tranquilizer. Her eyes felt gritty, and she heard phantom calls—Oldtooth's voice, Sula whimpering like an infant—and she whined and pulled against her bindings. With her jaws shut, the whine came out an off-key howl, a growl, and a squeak.

The woman in white was speaking. Her voice was more forceful than before as the man bent down with her. They were untying Marta's trusses.

The man finished loosening the ropes on Marta's feet while the woman peeled back the wolf's eyelids and dropped a salty liquid into them. The grittiness dissolved, and Marta spread her mouth in a yawn. The man and woman backed away suddenly when the wolf's smooth fangs stretched wide. The metal door clanged open and shut as they slipped out into the hall.

As Marta's senses slowly wound back to normal, she returned to her place against the wall. Ears back, eyes averted, her legs trembled ever so slightly. They remembered the urge to run, but for now, stillness was her protection. So she stayed, alive in her body but silent in her mind, until the voices came again the next day.

This time, the dimming was sudden and complete. She never saw the stick or felt the ropes, never heard the pulse of helicopter blades, never felt Oldtooth's and Sula's and Annie's warm bodies placed next to her. Never felt the earth fall away from underneath her or the altitude pop in her ears. Marta flew with her packmates, in the wide-eyed trance of chemical sleep, guided by unseen hands to an unknown destination.

SEVENTEEN

to run

This time when Marta awoke, the bindings were
gone. The whole bad dream was gone: the cement
slab, the metal cage, the bright lights, and confusing
smells were all gone. Only a trace of human scent lin-
gered, most of it from her own coat of fur.

And yet all was not right. Marta was outside and her
feet and jaws were free, but the land was wrong. She was
not home; this was not Pleasant Valley. Even with the
sky spinning above and the earth tilting below, the smells
told Marta she had never been here before. The plants,
the rocks, the water spelled out a location that could have
been five miles or five hundred miles from anything she
knew. She was free now, it seemed, but she was lost.

To make matters worse, the season was wrong.

Marta had last seen the sky in Pleasant Valley in the late glow of summer. These were mountains in the chill gray of earliest winter. Impossible: impossible to sleep that long. Impossible to travel in one's sleep. How long had she been in captivity? How did she get there? Where was she now? Wherever it was, it was not home. It was high and it was cold—and it stank of something fearful. Grizzly bear.

Bear! Marta's instincts scrambled to attention, but tangled with the chemicals still in her blood. The trees bent above her, and the gray clouds seemed to tumble under her feet. She felt as if she were being chased, then cornered, then chased again. She barked a warning bark but it came out a groan. Her eyes were gritty again, but this time there was no woman in white with soothing eyedrops.

Marta tripped over something and reared back, startled. Sula! The young wolf's face came in and out of focus as Marta felt the familiar teeth and tongue on her whiskers. Sula's whine reached her ears, but sounded wrong through the haze of tranquilizer. A second whine, a second mouth: Annie.

Images tumbled in Marta's head. The traps, the darts, the cages, lights, ropes, aircraft, voices, smells— the human scent clung to her, drowning out even the smell of her pups. She shook violently, but the alien scent remained.

Marta's legs throbbed. There were no block walls in front of her, and no wire fences on any side. The radio collar still hung around her neck, but her ankles were free. Gravity righted itself, and she felt her feet on the cold ground. Vaguely, she made out high cliffs on either side of a narrow valley, and the smell of bear filled her nostrils. Then her first instinct, the one that had always saved her before, poked into her mind: to run.

Marta ran.

She gathered her legs and bounded out of the clearing, soaring past Oldtooth's gray form. She ran down, with the flow of water. Down, toward warmth. Down, away from winter. Down toward deer, away from bear.

Down she went like the water rushing in Nyack Creek. Down, and away from the puzzled look on Annie's gray face. Down and away from where Sula whined, sniffing the cold wind and turning to lick at Oldtooth's sleeping muzzle. Down through the thickets of alder and aspen and thimble-berry. Down through the suffocating scent of grizzly bear. The creek bottom grew steeper, and Marta ran faster. The trail grew narrow, the alder closed in, and Marta still ran. The overcast sky grew dimmer as the sun dropped to the west, and

Marta ran on. As a pup, this was how she ran from danger. When her pack was poisoned, this was how she ran. She ran for her life.

As before, she had no idea where she was running. As before, she had no one to run with. Marta ran without thought or intention. She ran without food, without feeling, without stopping. She ran, simply ran.

EIGHTEEN

lost

Sula and Annie watched their mother disappear into the thickets. This was not the first time she had left them at a rendezvous site with Oldtooth. He was sleeping as usual, though his eyes were open in an unusual way. It was also unusual for Marta to leave without so much as a lick or a howl, but in the last few weeks, everything had been unusual.

Their bodies felt strange right now, after a very strange sleep. Their collars were not uncomfortable, fastened loosely around their necks as they had been in the clinic. This place was new too, but to the pups, almost everything was new.

One thing was familiar, and that was the feeling of hunger. Sula felt it as soon as she was awake. The black pup turned to Oldtooth and whined, sniffing at his long jaws. Oldtooth's nose twitched, but his eyes remained unseeing. She whined again, louder and longer.

After a moment, Oldtooth licked his lips. Sula's whine slid back into her throat and turned into a mournful, half-grown howl, and a faint light crept into the old wolf's eyes. His ears flicked forward and he half raised his head. He made to stand up, but his foreleg—the injured one—buckled under him and a wave of pain crossed his grizzled face. He slumped back to the ground.

Betrayed, Oldtooth looked down at the paw firmly taped in its white bandage. He bit feebly at it. Though still addled by the tranquilizer, he could tell that the tape was tight and strong, and his dull teeth would not pierce it.

A few feet away, Annie heard Oldtooth grunting irritably and wriggled over to help. She bit clumsily at the bandage with her growing teeth, and the first nip made her old friend yelp with pain. Annie tugged harder and Oldtooth yelped louder. His body jerked in a series of spasms, and he gave a warning bark that sounded strangely like a scolding. Annie drew back, surprised, and for several moments Oldtooth's eyes swam in and out of focus as the drug cleared from his mind. When he seemed quiet again, Annie leaned back toward him.

Sniffing at his foot, she gently licked at the dressing over his toes, then nuzzled his gray chin.

Sula, meanwhile, had been running excited laps around the clearing ever since Oldtooth raised his head. Now she veered out of her circuit and plopped down in front of her packmates, panting and licking both faces equally: first Oldtooth, then Annie, then Oldtooth again. The old wolf's blood rose at the feel of her sharp teeth on his mouth, and he fought to make sense of the sights and smells around him.

No cages, no cement. They were no longer in the bright place where all the rules were different from the way of the wolf. The flat gray sky stretched over them, and the wet earth was back underneath. But this was not the sky or the earth of Pleasant Valley.

This was a higher place, and a colder place. It was narrow, not broad, and thickly forested, with snowy crags jutting into the gray ceiling of clouds. The damp air carried a thousand subtle scents into Oldtooth's nose, but one was not so subtle, and it snapped his head to attention: bear. They were in grizzly country. Oldtooth let out a real warning grunt and turned to look for Marta.

Where was his hunting partner, the leader of their pack? The grasses were still flat where she had slept, but she was nowhere to be seen. Oldtooth threw back his head and howled in earnest. The pups howled too then, and the calling song brought him to his feet despite his bandage and wound.

Having roused her old friend at last, Sula leaped to her feet, singing high and clear into the cold sky. Annie joined in on the middle notes, and Oldtooth—still jangled by sleep—sometimes sang low and sometimes wavered off key. Nose to nose, their voices wove together as they sang the calling song, the hungry song, the lonesome song, and the lost song. But when they finished the only reply was their own echo, cascading down the snowy slopes of the gorge.

NINETEEN

trespassing

Nyack Creek grew bigger and noisier as it flowed downstream. The calls of Marta's pack were swallowed by the forest, and she heard nothing above the gurgling of water and the panting of her breath. She ran into the night, and where the smell of bear grew stronger, she ran faster. When she became thirsty, she ran into the creek to gulp its cold water. She did the only thing she knew how to do, run, in the only direction that made sense: down.

A century ago the Nyack Valley might have been a wolf highway, but it belonged to the grizzly bear now. Droppings and tree scrapes showed where one bear's range ended and the next began. The great bear was king of the food chain and the only animal, other than an angry moose, that Marta had to fear. She ran on alert, adrenaline pumping as she trespassed through the territory of beasts ten times her size.

Sometime after nightfall, Marta felt the trail level out. When she stopped to drink, she found the water broad and flat. Not far away, she heard the deep whisper of a river.

As Marta listened to the river she became aware of a much closer sound. It was coming from the opposite direction, upstream from where she stood. The splash sounded as though a big stone had fallen into the creek, but it was followed by another deep splash, and still another. Marta did not have to sniff the air; only one animal was big enough to make that noise. The stones in the creek clanked together under the grizzly's massive feet. The water hissed when he clawed its surface, fishing for salmon that—once plentiful—had become few.

Marta held her breath, stone still, hearing the bear's teeth clamp down on a small kokanee. Fish were food and her stomach was empty, but the sound did not make her want to eat; it made her want to run. She slipped away on the soft creek bank, leaving the sound of the bear behind her. Soon Marta came to the edge of the forest, where the creek flowed into the river. The flood plain was braided with gravel channels and shrubby hills that ran along the big water. At the main channel, she heard another rushing sound: there, above the far embankment, was a road. A smooth, hard road with cars that shot by in a rush of metal and oil. Big water and big road: both lay ahead of Marta at the end of Nyack Creek.

She could go no farther without being seen. Being seen had gotten her captured. Being seen had gotten Calef killed. She could not go back either; behind her were too many bears and the signs of winter.

Marta stood in the autumn night, toes to the icy waters of the Middle Fork of the Flathead River. No cars passed, and the low hum of the water soothed her. Her blood cleansed of the drug and her body exhausted, she ached with the need to sleep.

A car rushed past, but its headlights never touched the wolf shadow standing at the river's edge. No one saw the shadow drink from the river, turn, and disappear into the brush.

TWENTY

abandoned

After Marta left, Oldtooth came to his senses slowly. Sleep and waking fought back and forth inside him as he called for her, and when his last howl ended in a wheeze, he sank to the ground in defeat. Marta was gone, he was hurt, the pups were hungry, and he couldn't even sing.

His body was failing him, but that was nothing new. Bad teeth and a bad foot were only the start of his problems; these days, Oldtooth was having a hard time keeping track of himself. From Pleasant Valley to the clinic to here—wherever that was—he kept going to sleep in one place and waking up somewhere else. Nothing in the old wolf's experience could account for this.

Annie and Sula were too young to understand the strangeness of sleeping in one place and waking up in another. In the past months, they had gone from the darkness of the den to the playground of the forest, and from the shelter of the trees to the great skies of the meadow. Once they drank milk, and now they ate meat. Once they had no collars, and now they did. Once Oldtooth had no bandage, and now he did. The life of a wolf pup was full of changes.

On their own, the pups didn't know danger from safety or good from bad. Whenever they didn't know what to do, they followed their elders. Now, when they saw Oldtooth anxiously sniffing the air, they sniffed anxiously too—but the smell of bear meant little to them. So Annie and Sula did what wolf pups were supposed to do: play and beg for food.

Not that these two were looking so puppylike anymore. Their feet were almost as big as Marta's, and their ears no longer looked too large for their heads. Though half the size of Oldtooth and still weak from captivity, both youngsters had the strong, rangy silhouettes of adult wolves. Annie was the color of prairie grasses in a dry season, a dappled, feathered gray that rippled like the meadow of Pleasant Valley. Sula, like Marta, wore black fur over a silvery undercoat. Apart from more size, to be a full-fledged wolf all they lacked were teeth—and sense.

Annie's canine teeth were little more than hard spots

in her gums. Sula still had baby teeth, and they were getting loose. If there was any biting to be done here in the upper Nyack Valley—and there would be no hunting without a certain amount of biting—Oldtooth would have to do it.

Then there was the matter of sense. Though Annie and Sula had the proportions of grownups, they knew little of wolf ways. Wolves their age still needed to play monkey see, monkey do, tug-of-war, and hide-and-seek. They needed to watch from a distance while a pack of good hunters made every kind of kill, and they needed the meat from those kills to fill out their half-grown bodies. The young of the year needed to chase one another until their bones grew long and thick, and to practice every move until it came effortlessly: tracking, chasing, cornering, dodging, killing. They needed to play follow the leader for many seasons, until they learned the way of the wolf.

When their howl did not bring Marta and when Oldtooth sank back to the ground, the sisters were hungry enough to begin their own hunt around the clearing. Sula flushed a ptarmigan almost immediately, but sprang back in surprise. A wiser wolf would have sprung forward—getting, not spending, precious energy—but that was arithmetic. Sula hadn't learned arithmetic yet, and neither had Annie. What they did know was tag, so tag was what they played. Around and around the clearing they dashed. Despite the tranquilizers, the lack of food, and weeks of confinement, they played with zest. Annie zoomed in for nips at Sula's throat and shoulder, getting beat out—as sometimes she was, even before their capture—by her sister's rattlesnake speed.

Round and round they went, not noticing the strangeness of the place, the lateness of the season, or even, for the moment, their own hunger. Not noticing, until they finally stopped to rest, that Oldtooth was gone.

TWENTY-ONE

hungry for home

At first light, Marta was wakened by a steady drizzle patting the cottonwood leaves over her head. It was cold here, but not as cold as the high place she had run from. Blinking, she lifted her nose: there was the cold, fast river in front of her, and the trace of grizzly bear behind her.

Marta stood. Her eyes felt sandy and her joints stiff as she ducked out from the brush. She ached, and not just from the long run and the short sleep. For the first time since being captured, Marta was hungry, and it was not an ordinary hunger. Though she had eaten nothing in the past week, this discomfort was not in her belly but in every muscle, bone, vein, and shaft of fur. What she felt there, half-hidden in the cottonwood saplings on the

Middle Fork, was not a meat hunger. It was the hunger for home.

Home: the key to survival. In Pleasant Valley, for the first time in her life, she had lived as a wolf was meant to live, with a home and pack that were hers alone. In the nightmare that began when she found the first trap near the den site, Marta had lost both home and pack. She still had the will to live; that had been dimmed in the clinic, not destroyed.

To survive, Marta needed a home. Land was life itself; without the right habitat Marta could not even save herself.

Pleasant Valley was home. It fit. There, she knew how to hunt and she knew where to hide. There, she knew how to survive. Here, she knew she would not.

Two cars hurtled past on the highway. Marta crept to the riverbank, looking up and down the winding valley. This was not home. Wherever home was, she had found it before, and she would find it again.

Marta trotted to the river's edge, drank, and studied the surface of the water. Downstream were whitecapped rapids; upstream the water looked calm but fast. Marta ran upstream, ducking into the brush when she heard traffic on the road.

At a narrow point in the river, Marta stopped and gauged the crossing. It was many times her own length, and too deep to wade. A golden cottonwood leaf twisted in the eddies. Despite its gliding surface, the current underneath was strong.

Marta plunged in, and the cold swallowed her. Hard as she paddled, the river pushed her toward the rapids faster than she could push herself to the opposite shore. Straining to keep her chin above water, Marta refused to look downstream. Water swirled around her radio collar. With one ear to the growing roar of whitewater, she kept her eyes fixed on the rocky bank and pulled steadily toward it. She did not panic in the current, but let her body angle downstream as she paddled into the deepest part of the river.

Pull, pull. Pumping blood into her legs, which were almost numb from the cold, Marta felt the current begin to weaken as she neared the shore. The instant before her paws nicked bottom, a great roar filled her ears. Marta shot a look at the rapids, but their roar was still several lengths downstream. The new roar was coming not from the water, but from the shore in front of her.

The roar of the rapids or the roar from on shore: momentum sent Marta through the frigid water and dully, she felt her pads touch the river bottom. She dug in her claws and scrambled out of the current. The wall of noise slammed into her and she dropped, dripping, onto the smooth stones as a freight train clattered past on the tracks above her.

After the train passed, she peered up over the bank and looked along the tracks. She listened. No trains. No cars. The valley was silent except for two sounds: the rush of whitewater and the sound of a small airplane droning up the Nyack drainage she had just come down.

Marta sprang up the embankment, leaped the tracks, and was across the road before her coat had even stopped dripping. She did not pause on the other side; she could be seen there, and anyway, there was nothing to stop for.

There were no scent posts, no landmarks, no familiar trees or rocky outcrops by which to choose direction. Home, wherever it was, lay in the only direction Marta knew: straight ahead.

TWENTY-TWO

not quite alone

Sula stood panting in the middle of the clearing and turned a triumphant eye toward her sister. The race was over and she had won. Annie, panting too, gazed back levelly; win or lose, she was still the one to be answered to. The empty space in Sula's middle felt suddenly bigger, and she turned to beg food from Oldtooth's gray muzzle. Not there.

Sula's panting ended in a gulp. She ran to the spot where Oldtooth had been and whimpered, but no gray shape emerged from the bushes. She looked around. Suddenly the clearing seemed much bigger than it had, and new smells licked at her from every direction. Hunching her shoulders, she peered at the snowy peaks towering above.

Then without a glance at Annie, Sula threw back her

head and howled. It was a blunt, how-dare-you-leave-us-like-this howl. Marta was off somewhere, and now Oldtooth too. That just didn't happen, not this soon after moving to a new spot. Not when they were this hungry.

Sula's howl ended in a grunt, and she plopped to her belly in the spot where Oldtooth had lain. It was still warm. With a huff, she poked her black nose between her black paws and waited. Annie prowled the clearing, pretending to ignore her sister, but soon gave up and plopped down next to Sula. Side by side they lay, waiting for Marta or Oldtooth to come and show them what to do.

They waited, and noon became afternoon. They waited and their stomachs growled, and the wind picked up in the trees. They waited and dozed, and noises skittered in the brush near the creek. Finally, in the hour just before dark, Sula was wakened by an especially loud growl coming from her sister's direction. She reached over to nip Annie awake, but Annie was far from asleep. Ears back, neck tight, her nose pointed straight into an awful smell coming from the brush a few yards away. Whiskers trembling, the fur around Annie's gray neck ruffed out like Oldtooth's when he sensed danger. A new noise gnarled from her throat.

Sula swept to her feet with a fearful yip, and just then a crash sounded from the direction of the smell.

Grizzly bear. The harsh grunts and breaking of branches were coming their way. Though the pups had never seen a grizzly, instinct took over and they shot from their bed.

As they bounded away, an ancient bear with silvertip fur burst into the clearing. She stopped, snorting angrily at the mix of man and wolf scent, and cocked a pale ear after Annie and Sula. Their scent still fresh, the grizzly charged, crossing the grass in one smooth motion, but the wolves were already losing themselves in the thick brush above the clearing. The sow halted with a lurch. Unable to see what she could smell and hear, she swung her great head low and bellowed, creek water dripping from her chin.

The bear peered after the scared-puppy sounds fading into the brush, and clapped her jaws shut with an impatient snap. Just beyond her bad sight, a streak of gray and a streak of black vanished into the darkness as fast as their half-grown legs could carry them.

TWENTY-THREE

starburst

As the pups blazed a frightened trail upstream, their old friend and teacher limped haltingly in the opposite direction. When in danger, Oldtooth had the same urge to run as Marta, and when he left the clearing, his leaving was as sudden. He did not turn back to see Sula besting Annie in their game of tag, and there was no farewell howl or final wolf kiss. This was not arithmetic; it was reflex. The last weeks had tangled his intelligence like a clump of winter fur, and for now he moved on instinct alone. Like Marta, the command went to his feet and—despite the throb—they obeyed. Like Marta, he went downhill.

Oldtooth never heard Sula's indignant howl. By the time the pups noticed his absence, he was deep into the thick, beary brush of Nyack Creek. Though he left shortly after Marta, he was not catching up with her. The trail she left was narrow and fast, while his was looping and wide.

The old wolf was hurting. Despite the days of rest and care in the clinic, his paw was worse, not better. On rocky parts of the trail he flinched each time the foot touched the ground. He rested often, biting testily at the wrap and carefully cleaning his other three paws. He could not afford to lose any more.

Oldtooth traveled and rested, crossing Marta's scent and sign along the way. Although she had run straight through the grizzlies' territories, he made sharp detours around the bark scrapes that marked one bear's range from another. But then, Marta could run from danger. At this point, Oldtooth could barely walk.

He had lived through worse. The time in the coyote trap was worse. Between the steel teeth sawing into his leg bone and his bloody jaws sawing against the metal hinge, all that existed in those hours was pain. It consumed him so completely that he didn't notice when the trap broke open and kept on chewing. That was how he broke so many teeth.

The pain now in his paw was little by comparison. But it was enough, as Oldtooth made his way down the drainage of the Nyack, that it slowly dulled his wits. After a while he began to ignore the scrapes of short bears;

then the scrapes of larger bears; finally he ignored all sign of grizzly, and the loops and detours in his track shrank to a single, slow thread. All he could do was follow in Marta's tracks, one labored step after another.

By the time Marta reached the Middle Fork, Old-tooth had traveled half that far, and the pups were running headlong in the opposite direction. Scattered like a starburst, the Pleasant Valley pack was a pack no more.

TWENTY-FOUR

hungry horse

Having escaped whitewater, trains and cars at the river, Marta turned into the mountains on the south side of the highway. Under a cold, needle-fine rain, she ran up an avalanche chute that gave her a clear trail and a trickle of water to drink. Near the top of Pyramid Peak the drizzle hardened into sleet, and the cliff face was slicked over with ice. Marta scrambled up the bluff in bursts, gripping the ice with her claws. She slipped once, pushing loose a head-size boulder that bounced down the avalanche chute like a skull.

Marta caught her footing again and stood, sides heaving. She could hear the wind and snow driving over the crest, and something in it smelled good, like a valley. Like home. She settled her feet, caught her breath, and plunged for the top.

On the summit she was greeted with a gust of wind that nearly sent her rolling down after the boulder. With it came a biting blast of snow, and Marta wrinkled her nose and shook. When she opened her eyes, she peered into the distance.

What she saw was mist and snow. Her nose was not wrong; there was a valley below. She inhaled, getting a chestful of snow along with the scent. It was a valley with trees and deer and—Marta's ruff raised slightly— bear. But there was more: big water, much bigger than Dahl Lake. Big water, bear, and no meadow. This was not Pleasant Valley.

Marta shook the snow from her black overcoat and stepped down from the ridge, toward the big water. The snow mixed with rain as Marta descended, and by the time she reached the water's edge, both had stopped. The overcast was breaking open, and the last of the sun slanted through ragged clouds. It would be night soon.

As Marta rested in a grove of trees by the shore of Hungry Horse Reservoir, the first stirrings of meat hunger mixed with her hunger for home. Though she had not eaten for over a week, and had eaten badly for weeks before that, she was too tired to bring herself to hunt. She tended her feet instead, all four in turn, nip- ping gravel from between the pads and licking ice scratches on the skin. Usually the pack did this together, playing or napping before going on with their journey.

But Marta had no pack now, no one to play with and no urge to nap. Paws tended, she felt a pang and then a song rising from inside, pulling her to her feet and pointing her nose at the sky. She was lost and hungry, but that wasn't what she sang. She needed to hunt, but she did not sing that either. She would have called for her pack, but she could not sing that far. She sang the only song she could: the lonesome song. She sang it long, and when the notes died away she sang it again. In the silence a single star, the first of the night, winked out from behind the parting clouds.

Exhausted, hungry, she picked up one paw and placed it in front of the others. Her feet were the only way home.

TWENTY-FIVE

black wolf, black water

Under a dark, clearing sky, Marta followed the road along the shore of the reservoir. As she rounded a curve, she heard a disturbance. The glow of a bonfire lit a circle of trees, and in the circle were dozens of people: young people, some jumping about and playing and others sitting and staring at the fire. The loud ones were hooting and shouting, and above their voices howled a strange metallic voice with a metallic, pounding heartbeat.

Marta stopped, her own heart pounding against the music. Intent on the danger in front of her, she did not notice a danger from behind. Coming around the curve, tires scraping gravel, a car was upon her before she knew it.

The flash of headlights caught only her hind legs and

a swish of tail as she lunged left, off the gravel and into the narrow band of trees between the road and the water. Marta crouched there, turning her head and squeezing her eyes shut against the rock fragments spinning out from the back tires. Marta heard the pounding of the car's own metallic heartbeat, and a cloud of exhaust bloomed around her. Before it could settle she was back on the road, looking for a way around the party. The smell of metal and oil was strong from the string of cars that lined the road up and down from the fire.

The car that nearly hit Marta pulled up and stopped at the end of the row. The driver got out and slammed the door shut, a clank of metal on metal that made Marta jump. She froze, but both driver and passenger moved away from her and toward the people silhouetted against the blaze of their bonfire.

Now another car approached from behind, more slowly than the first, and the wolf again ducked into the shadows. As the second car slowed and parked another started, filling the air with burned-oil smell. It spun around, back in Marta's direction.

The black wolf hunched motionless. It was not safe to go on, but she had come too far to turn back. She wanted to go onward, forward, ahead. She wanted to go home.

Marta left the road and crept down to the reservoir's edge. Shadows of the bonfire glazed her coat, and golden sparks mixed with stars in the calm, black water. This was big water, indeed: to her right and left, as far as she could see, the shore ribboned in and out of bays and peninsulas.

Marta stepped in and drank. This water was cool, and it felt good on her mountain-weary paws. It smelled simple: no oil, no metal, just the freshness of night. Marta sank into the water and began to swim.

The water was not as cold as the river had been, and Marta swam easily, with no current to pull her off course. Her black head and neck made black ripples in the water, and the stars and sparks twinkled in her wake as she swam away from shore.

From the water, Marta saw the cut-out shape of mountains on the opposite shore. Both sight and smell told her they were a long swim away, and nothing told her what else might lie on the other side. The night was calm, and the water was big—even bigger than she had pictured from the top of the ridge. Running all the way around it would have been hard on her sore paws. She swam.

Marta swam steadily as the stars cut their circles overhead. The mountains in front of her got bigger as the mountains behind got smaller. She swam without tiring, though she still had not eaten. The only discomfort came through her wet fur: the chill of the water, growing colder as it got deeper, was making its way into her muscles. The fat she had built up during the few good weeks of summer was long gone, and underwater, her coat was little protection from the cold.

When Marta was halfway across the reservoir, she picked out the shortest route to land. Cold or not, now there would be no turning back.

The chill sank deeper into Marta's body as she continued. By now a light wind had come up from in front of her, and little waves clapped at her throat as she paddled onward, chin high, radio collar soaked, into the new breeze. Gradually the stars disappeared from the water, erased by waves. Marta paddled on.

The breeze grew stronger then, and the waves lapping at her throat began to break around her shoulders. Before long she was going through the waves, not over them, and catching her breath in between. The mountains beckoned, but Marta's progress was hindered by bigger waves and rougher wind.

Marta tore into the whitecaps. The bigger they got, the harder she swam. Her muscles were completely chilled now, and only the fiercest paddling kept the cold from sinking further into her bones. The mountains were taking forever to come near, but Marta no longer noticed the shore. Now she only noticed each wave.

The waves turned to small rollers, and she could no longer crash through them. Now she had to swim up and over one small hill after another. Marta noticed nothing but the next hill, though her feet were numb and the cold made her chest ache. Over this hill. Over the next hill. The image of land was gone from her mind. All that existed was one black wave, another black wave, and gulps of air in between.

Suddenly Marta crashed into something solid. She hit full force and sank for an instant, then came up snorting for air. She thrashed in the black water, trying to stay afloat, when she noticed a huge shape towering over her.

A tree. She had reached land. In her numbness, she had not felt the water grow warmer as the rocky bottom rose to meet the shore. The last wave had slammed her into an underwater stump, cutting a gash in her chest.

Marta dragged herself up onto the bank, heaving for air. Numb, she could not feel the ground under her paws. Her head felt distant from her body, and she could not feel that her ribs were bruised and her chest was bleeding.

Marta shook weakly and lost her balance, tumbling to her side on the clay bank. She picked herself up and inched toward cover. Light was growing in the east, behind the mountains she had come from, and she could not sleep where she could be seen. She half slid and half crept up the shore, a shadow in the first light of dawn. She collapsed in the shelter of a brilliant red huckleberry bush.

TWENTY-SIX

salmon fishing

I t took days of old wolf persistence and some luck, but Oldtooth finally reached the Middle Fork, as Marta had, without having to fight any bears. In other ways, though, his luck was not holding.

Alone, he could not feed himself. The deer and elk of the Nyack were too big for his broken teeth, and the ptarmigan and hare were too fast for his injured foot. Unlike Marta, who was young enough and strong enough to put off hunger for a few more days, by the time Oldtooth arrived at the river, he craved meat from the middle of his belly to the tips of his guard hairs.

When he discovered the decaying body of a beaver rolled up on the riverbank, he lunged into it with a fever. Too hungry to drag the carcass into the trees, he stood in plain sight of cars swishing by on the highway and downed the stinking meat in gulps. His gray flanks blended with the dusty blues and pinks of the river rocks in a natural camouflage, and he fed undisturbed.

Hunger appeased for now, Oldtooth staggered into the brush and slept. After a few hours he wakened and spent the rest of the day wandering this way and that along the banks of the Middle Fork. If he was looking for another beaver carcass, he looked in vain; most animals were still fat and strong from summer, and pickings were not easy.

The next day, his hunger returned and quickly got the best of him. Ignoring the usual scent tracks, chasing everything from snakes to water ouzels, Oldtooth's arithmetic was reduced to one crucial formula: eat or die. The shorter days triggered his wintering urge, and the old wolf turned downstream, picking his way along the dry flood beds of the river.

The river rocks, though smooth, made him more lame, and he covered only a mile or two at a time. When he stopped to rest he tugged at the bandage on his foot, but it had been bound with skill and loosened only slowly. The looser he made it, the more his foot swelled. His limp grew worse. The muscles in his foreleg gave out, and the bandage grew frayed and dirty.

Oldtooth would have died there, by the river, but for one thing: salmon. The slow-minded kokanee, making their way upstream to spawn, were heart-red and easy to see in the clear water. Oldtooth discovered he could hunt them without running, without even standing, lying motionless where a swirl of current brought the salmon close to shore. Snatching a fish with his jaws, he would snap its spine with a whack on the stones. The smaller ones he swallowed whole.

Despite his fishing, within days after the Nyack Creek drop-off Oldtooth's condition had become desperate. Without proper food, he had little hope of healing. Already one toe had sloughed off inside the dressing, and the edges of pain were growing ominously dull. When the old wolf finally chewed through the tape, his foot had no life in it. An evil scent rose from the tissue, and from then on the smell went everywhere with him. It was the smell of any dead thing.

Moving on three legs, the old wolf continued downstream. He took some comfort from the icy waters of the Middle Fork, standing with his injured paw in the stream as he watched for schools of fish. Though the salmon arithmetic was not promising, at least it was a plus. There were no traps, no cages, no more bindings or drugged dreams. Where he lay down to sleep was where he woke up next.

One morning he woke to a strangely familiar scent. It was the smell of easier days, of pasture and cattle, and it was coming from the other side of the river. He found a smooth place to swim across and then limped gamely up a forested slope to the highway.

Across the road the pastures were still green and surrounded by thick trees. The breeze was full of cow smell, which would have made Marta's nose wrinkle, but didn't bother Oldtooth. After waiting for several cars to pass, he hobbled across the road and into the trees. Within moments, he caught his first mouse. There was good shelter in the underbrush, and good water in the creeks running through to the Middle Fork. The valley soil was flat and soft under his bad foot. Oldtooth stopped, and stayed. He would travel no farther.

TWENTY-SEVEN

first snow

Annie and Sula hid from the silvertip sow not one night, but many. Each time they waited until she was out of hearing, then made their way back to the clearing where they had last seen Marta and Oldtooth. Always before, if both adult wolves left the rendezvous site, one or the other returned shortly, but the days went by with no sound, no sign. For most of a week the pups stayed close to the drop point, making meals of any small creature that happened by, and learning to run at the first scent of the bear.

As hunger pulled at their bellies, they tried for larger meals—a snowshoe hare, a marmot—but nothing quite kept the flesh on their still-growing bones. Each night they returned to the rendezvous, howled their help song and hunger songs, and huddled together under the trees.

One night in the darkness, as Annie and Sula slept flank to flank, the cold drizzle falling around them began to crystallize in midair. The valley grew strangely silent, strangely soft, and by the time morning came, a change had come over the world.

Annie wakened first. Even when they had been tiny pups in the den, she was the first one awake and the first to go exploring. Lately, Sula was even slower than usual to wake up and follow her.

Overnight, a sprinkling of star-shaped crystals had frozen to Annie's face and, mystified, she pawed at her eyes. The stuff stuck to her back too, but her undercoat was not ready for winter, and the chill went to her skin. She stood up and shook fiercely, spraying flakes in a shower, then blinked at the scene before her.

The clearing was transformed. Curious, she ventured out to see what white powder had, magically, dusted their world overnight. Tiptoeing from the firs, she sniffed at the whiteness on the ground, but jerked back in surprise when flakes of ice flew into her nose. She snorted loudly, then sneezed. The sneeze woke Sula, who pawed her own eyes clear to watch Annie's experiment. For the moment, their hunger was replaced by fascination.

Annie stuck her nose back into the snow, this time on purpose. She burrowed down to the grass and inhaled deeply. Satisfied that the earth was still there, she flipped a clump of snow into the air and watched it fall. It exploded on impact, and she did it again, this time nosing a larger clump and flinging it higher.

Playtime! Sula ran to join Annie, but skidded to a stop when the first shock of snow hit her paws. Bewildered, she picked up one black foot after another, trying to keep them all off the ground at once.

Seeing Sula's dance, Annie chose the moment to tackle her. The two went down in the snow, wrestling for a hold on the other's neck until they were thoroughly soaked. When Annie had won—though Sula was faster, Annie was still stronger—Sula slipped the tackle and began to race around the clearing.

It was a race without reason. She ran and ran. The running instinct was there, but Sula had not learned that she needed something to run to, or at least from, for running to be worthwhile. So the thin black wolfling streaked around and around the clearing, a heedless chase headed straight toward starvation.

Annie stood, barking wildly from the center of her sister's erratic circles. When Sula would not stop, the gray wolf dropped belly first into the icy crust and lay, nose between her paws, whining to herself and watching with yellow, hungry eyes.

After a time the ache in Annie's belly sent a decisive

message to her feet, and she sprang up from the ground with a shake. Coming in at an angle, she thundered forward and bowled her sister over, then took off uphill. Sula rolled to her feet and took up the chase. Quickly the black shape overtook the gray, and soon they were both running, still without reason, up and up instead of around and around. The scent of their leaders muted under the new snow, the pups ran and ran: away from the rendezvous, away from their waiting, away.

TWENTY-EIGHT

not home

Exhausted from crossing the reservoir, Marta slept fitfully under her huckleberry bush. The sun had barely warmed her wet coat when she was startled by the clang of car doors above her. Groping for consciousness, the wolf cowered in her thicket as voices sifted down from the road. The numbness was gone, and in its place a piercing ache that centered in her chest and spread throughout her body. Marta creaked to her feet as painfully as Oldtooth ever had. Then she edged away from the noise, moving stealthily through the trees along the shore.

When the voices were out of hearing, she ducked across the road and, joints straining, picked her way up the mountainside. This was the hard way—but the easy way was blocked by people. She could not afford to be seen.

The ache in Marta's flesh sank into a dull weariness as she climbed her second range of mountains in as many days. Her energy was failing. She would have to eat soon, before she lost the strength to hunt. But still the search image in her mind was not an animal: it was a place. Home. The picture of Pleasant Valley lay in her mind's eye, with its great meadow, trickling creeks, and meandering deer tracks.

Marta reached the ridge by midafternoon, after a struggle through the steep puzzles of alder that grew up in old clear-cuts around the reservoir. At the top, Marta found herself overlooking the immense panorama of the Flathead Valley. To the north and west as far as she could see, the autumn fields basked under a hazy afternoon sun. Stretching to the south, under a gauze of blue, lay the calm waters of Flathead Lake.

Not Dahl Lake. Not Pleasant Valley. It was not home, but Marta ran toward it anyway. She ran down the steep and she ran through the thick. She ran the trails of elk and deer and even bear, animals scattering at her crashing, careless sound. She ignored scrapes on her paws and the wound on her chest and ran: down a rock slide, through more alder, and across the milky swirls of Noisy Creek.

By sunset, she reached the base of the mountains and began traveling along a foothill road toward the lake. Lights blinked on across the Flathead Valley, outlining the city of Kalispell, and the foothills came alive with warm sparks of light from outlying homes. Marta kept to the dark, and ran.

Marta ran for a week. She ran to Flathead Lake, but it was too cold to swim. She ran to the foothills, but they were full of homes. She ran to the valley, but it was busy with roads. She ran to the forests, but they ran out in clear-cuts. She ran all the way around Swan Lake and ended up where she started. Everywhere she went, she kept to the edges, just out of sight.

As her meat hunger grew, she hunted on the run. She caught just enough to keep alive: a grouse here, a rabbit there, a surprised fawn with its spots nearly gone, but no real food. Deer were plentiful in the northern Swan Valley, but so were roads and people. She could not hunt and hide at the same time. She needed a place where she could eat and sleep and not be seen. The ache in her chest and bones was blurred by fatigue. Her strength slipped away with each ridge she ran.

Marta tried every trail in her hunt for home. She ran the Swan Valley and back. She covered the east hills of Flathead Lake in detail, as though their rocky outlooks would show her the way. She ran the southern length of the Mission Mountains in a single day, but some strange tug—like the pull she had felt to her pack—called her back north. She ran in circles, in ovals, in straights, and in knots, stopping only to hide and sometimes sleep. She ran and ran and ran.

One night she left the foothills long after dark. The homes and streets were quiet as she passed the river near the sleeping village of Bigfork. Part of the river flowed through a building and made a loud hum there, spilling down a smooth stone chute before joining the rest of the channel below.

No cars appeared as she loped along the highway, and no dogs caught her scent from the yards in town. She trotted by old log buildings and new condominiums. She heard the Swan River growling hungrily below her as she crossed the old steel bridge and smelled hot grains baking in the cool night. The only light in downtown Bigfork came from the kitchen of the bakery. Marta sniffed deeply at the smell, but kept to the shadow as she passed.

Marta crossed the street, still in darkness, and made it to the highway just as a siren tore into the evening. The wolf dove for cover and a patrol car sped past, lights flashing and tires whining. She slunk deeper into the barrow pit and sneaked among the summer homes along the shore, headed south.

The rest of the night and the next day, she continued south along the lakeshore. She ran and hid, hid and ran. At one place she crouched for hours under a dock, waiting for a picnic to end before she could move on. Finally the houses thinned out, and at the end of the day she found herself on a deserted stretch of shoreline. She crept into the trees and rested, waiting for darkness. When dusk came, she inched out onto the gravel beach.

As she stood, the sunset deepened from gold to red across the long plate of glassy water, and Marta's energy ebbed with the light. In the past weeks she had survived chase and capture in Pleasant Valley. She had seen the world and seasons turned upside down, and suffered the loss of home and pack. For days she had traveled in hunger and pain, feeling little, hunting for home. Now, as the evening sky deepened from palest blue to indigo, Marta felt the end of her strength.

She felt the hunger now, and she felt the pain. She felt the gash in her chest, warm and swollen, and she felt her knees buckling beneath her. A chill swept through her body. With one last effort, she climbed back up the gravel shore and into the trees. The last thing she saw as her eyes sank shut was the glint of moonrise on a golden leaf, falling silently to the ground.

TWENTY-NINE

beaver woman lake

The day the snow fell, Sula followed Annie far upstream. They didn't know that the higher they went, the harsher the weather would be, or that the higher they went, the less there would be to eat. Rattled by hunger, with no leader to follow, the youngsters did not know how to use what sense they had.

As Annie and Sula continued upstream, they moved out of bear country and into the jaws of winter. The weather roused their urge to hunt, but instinct without teeth was as good as no instinct at all. The kind of prey they could catch and kill with milk teeth—in Annie's case, gums—was not what they needed. They needed meat, and plenty of it; they needed hunting practice, and plenty of it; they needed the protection of elders and pack. They had none.

While Oldtooth limped across a cow pasture far to the south and Marta ran mountain ranges far beyond that, in the wintry reaches of the Nyack one gray and one black wolf stopped growing. Annie's gray coat wore thin, and her stomach hurt all the time. Sula lagged farther behind, breathing hard when she ran and howling with a crack in her voice. Her milk teeth fell out, but no real teeth grew in. She ran less and rested more. Each day Sula grew more listless and sleepy, until one morning, even Annie's fiercest hunting howl did not rouse her.

Annie tried several times to wake her sister: first a nudge from her chin, then a wail, then an emphatic nip below the ear. Sula's whiskers did not even twitch.

The hunger in Annie's belly was deafening. She stood over Sula and bellowed, a tuneless song that swelled over her sister's back, still curled in sleep. Annie clamped her jaws around Sula's in a big sister wolf kiss, but still Sula's eyes didn't open. Her muzzle felt strange: strange and cold.

Annie cocked her head, sniffing gingerly. A strange smell—or lack of smell—came from the familiar black nose. Annie caught her breath and backed off stiffly. There in the cold, eyes fixed on her sister, Annie took the slowest of breaths. She held it for a moment, then let go. A faint mewl, like the cry of a newborn, rose on a trickle of steam from her lips.

Against logic, instinct undone, Annie pushed still farther upstream after Sula's death. Sometimes racing with panic and sometimes sluggish with fatigue, she crisscrossed the drainages of the upper Nyack. Along the way she snatched up rodents and sometimes ground birds, but nothing filled the howling in her belly. Her trek drew higher and higher into the stony peaks, until she came to Beaver Woman Lake. Like Sula, she became sleepy and listless, and she found shelter in a hollow between two dwarf fir trees.

It was quiet there, at Beaver Woman Lake, except for the falls humming down into the Nyack. There were no grizzly bears to run from, and the deer and elk had also moved down country for the season. For the first time in her short life, Annie was completely alone.

Soon she stopped feeling much of the cold, and her sense of smell dimmed. Her nerves carried only one message, hunger, but even that disappeared after a few days. She stopped hunting, and no longer moved except to wobble to the lake for a drink. Then she returned to her fir trees and rested. She listened to the tiny animals burrowing for winter, and she listened to the creeks spilling down the smooth cliffs of the cirque. The last sound she heard was the drone of a small airplane somewhere overhead, and it lulled her into a sleep from which she never wakened.

THIRTY

a few golden days

As fall made its way down to Nyack Flats, Oldtooth limped after rabbits and mice on the soft leaves of the forest floor. He had not been this hungry in years, not since the drought into which he was born. Constant hunting was all that kept him alive, and even so, his weight was falling. He became bolder, venturing out of the trees and into the pastures to chase small animals darting among the cattle herd.

Oldtooth grew sick. A fever rose and fell as he hunted, and the pain throbbed from what was left of his foot. He moved little, resting often. As flesh and bone fell away, there was nothing he could do but pull off the rotting toes. The pain was flat now, and he gave only a grunt as he bit at his flesh. It was a ghastly contrast to the real food he needed.

As Oldtooth's condition grew more grave, the smell of the cattle grew more tantalizing; livestock had saved his life in the north, and the taste for meat remained in his dull, cracked teeth. But these days he was no match for a full-size cow.

One night, the old wolf had been out in the pasture for several hours. Awkward on three legs and feverish, he tracked and lunged, lunged and tracked. Mouse, rabbit, or ground squirrel—it didn't matter; he snapped at everything. When he came upon a small steer that had strayed to the edge of the herd, his reaction was auto-matic. He lunged.

He caught the animal in the throat. The steer didn't have time to look; the big gray animal had been limping through the pasture for days, never giving the cattle more than a curious glance. Now Oldtooth had its neck in the blunt trap of his jaws, crushing windpipe and spine in one stroke. The animal fell, and Oldtooth gnawed blindly at its belly until he finally broke through the hide.

Oldtooth feasted that night. He devoured the organs and most of the flesh, then hobbled back to the woods to sleep. The next day he rested, somewhat revived, but when he went back to the carcass, it was mysteriously gone. In its place was the sharp tang of metal and the smell of strange wolf. Even in distress, Oldtooth would not be taken by traps again. He could taste the metal in his broken teeth. He skirted the trap and returned to the trees. His fever had dropped, and he almost chased a mouse as he entered the forest. Several nights later Old-tooth went back to the cow pasture, not wanting to lose the full feeling between his ribs. He killed again, and feasted again.

For a few autumn days in the Middle Fork Valley, Oldtooth savored what was left of his wolf life. Without pack or pups his pleasures were few, but he took them as he could. The hunger softened and pain dulled, he slept each day until the low sun arced over the mountains behind him. Waking to crisp air scented with golden poplar and aspen leaves, he limped through the hills above and the river below at an easy pace. In a safe hollow of the Middle Fork he would sun himself on the open rocks, out of sight of the highway, tasting the breezes that blew through the valley.

So Oldtooth endured for the time that was his. Then one cool afternoon when he was in the pasture, a vehicle pulled up and stopped. The door opened quietly, one metallic click followed by another sliding snap. The old wolf heard neither. Standing at the edge of the trees, his ears were tuned to the low conversation of the cattle and the rustle of leaves dropping quietly behind him.

With Marta now lost to the south and Annie and

Sula miles to the north, the wolf who had been their packmate, protector, and teacher stood for a moment, framed by trees, mountain, and afternoon sun. Suddenly there was a sharp noise in the fall air, another noise that changed everything, and at the edge of pasture, Oldtooth lay down for the last time. His arithmetic was done.

THIRTY-ONE

marta's dream

In her moonlit bed by Flathead Lake, Marta sank into unconsciousness. Sleep shut her eyes and slowed her heart. It stilled the muscles that had carried her over mountains and across water. The earth pulled heavily on her, and she settled deeper into her forest bed, drawn by the feathery force of gravity. Her breathing grew long and even. The moon glittered higher, the air grew cooler, and the dark breeze rattled papery leaves in the aspen trees. Larch needles fell in a rain, sprinkling Marta's back like a dusting of golden snow.

She did not stir. Neither the moon nor the breeze nor the sound of the highway could disturb a sleep so deep.

As Marta slept, she began to dream. First she dreamed a spring day in Pleasant Valley, playing in the sugary snow with Calef and Oldtooth. Then she dreamed the birth of the pups in her dark den, and her tail thumped the ground lightly. She dreamed the noise that changed everything, and the hungry days after Calef's death, and she whined through her teeth. She dreamed the hunting days of summer, and her whiskers quivered in the silvery darkness.

Then she dreamed the capture and the clinic and the Nyack, and her last glimpses of Rann, Oldtooth, Sula, and Annie. The whine turned to a half howl, and her feet strained as if running all the way back to them. But the howl ended in a gulp and Marta's body went limp, as if her life had ended. Her legs did not move, and her chest did not rise or fall.

After a long stillness she heaved a big breath, a sigh that let more air out than in, and fell into an even deeper sleep. The moon walked across the sky, and the shadows of leaves played across Marta's back. She drifted into the sleep of the dreamless.

The moon had nearly set, and the sky was frosty black above when a star fell. A blaze of white shredded the sky from north to south, lighting the backs of the mountains. Silent now, Marta slept the sleep of the very old or very young, and did not waken.

The sun rose and the highway grew noisy, and still she did not waken. The autumn day grew bright and warm, and Marta slept on. By afternoon a late storm rolled in across the lake, drenching both shores in rain and pounding the valley with hail. Water dripped from the trees, mixing with the dust and larch needles on Marta's fur, and still she slept. When a gust of wind splintered a dry pine on the ridge above, the wolf's body jerked but did not rise.

All the sleep she had not slept, all the food she had not eaten, all the miles she had not rested now weighed her down. She slept until the rain ended and her fur dried. She slept until the sky cleared again and deepened, and the moon peered over the mountains behind her.

In the calm, she dreamed once more. Marta dreamed again, but not of Pleasant Valley. Instead, she dreamed a valley even bigger and more beautiful: a place with deer bounding from every draw, with creeks and hollows, with sweet air and sun. If there were people, they passed lightly, and all that moved overhead were clouds.

Marta dreamed herself in this place, and in the dream she was surrounded by a pack. But the pack she knew was gone, and in its place were four, then five, then six youngsters, black and gray, all nipping at her muzzle. She saw a set of adult tracks, bigger than any paw print she had seen in life, leading from the rendezvous site. Finally, she dreamed a fullness in her belly, a fullness she had not known since Calef's death. A strong, wise feeling spread between her ribs, and her breathing deepened.

Marta's dream settled into her sleeping muscles and bones. It was a dream of home, a new home, and it stirred her thin blood. But still she slept. In the last rays of the moon, now a silky ripple on the surface of Flathead Lake, a black wolf slept under clusters of white-berried buckbrush and did not move.

PART THREE

THIRTY-TWO

counting coup

When Marta wakened, she sprang to life. As if by magic, after the long sleep and dreams, her ears were forward and her tail high as they had not been for weeks. Her chest throbbed slightly, but no heat came from the wound. She seemed in command of herself, and the alpha look burned again in her eyes. She could not save her pack now, but perhaps she could save herself. She took a long drink of the autumn air. It tasted new.

The look in her eye and the lift in her nose said one thing: Marta was hungry. After weeks with little food, her cheeks were sunken, and hipbones poked through her ragged fur. The appetite she had lost was back, and more. Her hunger for home was drowned out by a surging hunger for meat. Without food, the fire in her eyes would not last long; she had little time before disaster or disease would set in.

For now, Marta did not need a home. With no pack to feed and protect, she would not need a real home until spring—and then only if she found a mate. Marta had no interest in a mate. Her one interest was food, and it pushed her like a stiff wind off the lake. Whatever instincts had kept her here were gone now, faded with the images from her last dream, and she left the busy Flathead area for good.

Heading south and east, Marta discovered that the Swan Valley was overrun with whitetail deer, her prey of choice. She also discovered that she was too weak to hunt them. Though her spirit was back, her speed was not, and she would have to build her strength with smaller, less demanding meals.

Marta hunted as she explored. On the trail she snapped at the smallest creatures, and no ground squirrel was safe in her path. Once she bit at a bright flash of fur before realizing, with a yelp, that what she had attacked was a flash of sunlight on her own front paw.

As the only wolf for hundreds of miles, Marta had little competition. In the generations since the wolf had been driven out, the deer had flooded in, and the margins of the Swan Highway were a boneyard of their losses. Hungry enough to risk being seen, Marta made meals of the more recent roadkills. She ate fast, ready to run from the cars that sped by day and night. The smell of metal and oil hung over the highway, keeping her on edge.

Marta had not seen her pack members die, but instinct no longer pulled her toward their old home. Hunger pulled her now, and so did the season. Fall had come, and with it came the urge to travel. Deer and elk were on the move to winter range, and in a wolf pack, by now the young of the year could almost keep pace with the adults. Marta's young were gone, and she ran as if to make up for the whole pack, covering ten, twenty, and even fifty miles in a day. Driven by a force deeper than flesh or bone, she covered the smooth Swan Range to the east, the craggier Mission Mountains to the southwest, and the long valley in between. Her meat hunger came back quickly now; her speed did not.

One day when Marta wakened, fullness was the only thing that mattered. Nested in the foothills below Red Owl Mountain, she did not feel the cold nip in the air. When a truck crunched by on nearby gravel, she did not hear it. A shot rang out in the distance, but she did not react. Her fear of being seen was gone for now, and all that remained was hunger: the kind of hunger that pulled life from death.

Marta rose from her nest and stretched her neck into a long, slow hunting howl. A trace of steam rose into the morning chill. She shook herself from nose to tail, then loped off. She pursued one deer track after another, but now that rifle hunting season had started, the animals were skittish. Intent on filling her belly this time, she ignored smaller animals and bone piles, and her hunger rose with the sun.

By afternoon, Marta found herself on a hiker trail in an old forest burn. She ran recklessly, exposed to view on the fire-shaved hillside, but still found no prey to test. Near the top of Red Owl, exhausted and empty, she dropped to her belly on a rocky outcrop. She was still panting when she heard the jubilant cackle of ravens.

Marta stopped panting. Ravens were her longtime helpers from the animal world: during hard times in the north, the big, black birds had led her to many meals. The very sound of their voice made her mouth water. Marta rolled to her feet and leaped down from the outcrop in one bound. Sun danced on the whiskers of her nose. Her black mane ruffled against the radio collar, touched by a warm autumn wind. Marta scanned the valley for the birds.

The sound was coming from below, not far into the steep drainage below Red Owl. The hunting look flickered in Marta's eyes, and she ran downhill as quickly and silently as she had come up. Within moments she was at the top of a scree slide, listening intently in each direction.

No ravens spoke. She jogged right to avoid the scree spurs under her paws, but a strong scent made her stop. A cluck sounded from above, and she whirled around. There, up slope, were the watching ravens—and there, under the ravens' feet, were the exploded remains of a mule deer. In life it had been a big animal, a five-point prize that would have meant honor to the bow hunter who brought it home. In death, to Marta, it meant one thing: survival.

Marta bounded toward the food. The ravens took off in a storm of protest, and were out of the way when the wolf suddenly came to a halt. One smell towered over the musk of dead deer, and that was the smell of bear. Though the buck died from the arrow broken in its chest, the carcass had been claimed by a large and bad-smelling grizzly bear. This time of year it would be an irritable, hungry bear as well.

Marta halted, but only for an instant. The bear was nowhere in sight, and she fell upon the meat. The organs were already taken, so she stripped the hide off the back-strap and ribs. She devoured the flesh, taking such slabs of muscle and fat that they bulged the sides of her neck as she swallowed. She was too hungry to chew. In moments her shrunken stomach was hurting for a new and welcome reason, and Marta kept gorging. She broke lustily into the ribs, savoring the crack of bones under her strong, white teeth.

Marta was saved. The past weeks had pushed her to the brink of exhaustion, and she needed nothing so much as a filling meal—especially one she didn't have to chase. Weak as she was, Marta could never have taken down a deer this big. She crunched into a second section of rib bones.

The crunch in her ears was loud, but the roar of the bear behind her was even louder. Marta choked and coughed out a spray of bone. She didn't need to see the face that went with that growl; both loomed over her, and she sprang away from the sound.

A few steps away, she glanced back at the bear. He was enormous. His golden fur shimmered with the rumble in his chest. Marta still had time to run for safety, but something stopped her: the taste of the meat still on her tongue. She had a blood tie here, a survival pact with this carcass, and she was not going to turn tail now. A coyote would have; a different wolf might have; in less desperate times, even Marta might have run. This time, she stood her ground.

The bear had Marta on size, but she drew on the last of her speed. He reared above her, long claws sticking out like a giant sunburst from his forefeet. Marta kept low, growling up at the waving paws. As he dropped to the ground, Marta backed away, barking and snapping at his massive feet. The bear reached out to swat her, and one claw kissed the end of her nose. Marta dodged down slope—a harder angle for the bear to follow—and before he could see what was happening, she veered uphill, headed for his backside.

It was a sight that Red Owl Mountain had not seen for a hundred years: a hungry black wolf making a run at an angry grizzly bear. He was fat from a month of huckleberries; she was thin from a month of hardship. The wolf could not kill the bear, but she could make it known, with the point of her teeth, how much she needed this meat.

Marta counted coup on the grizzly bear. To count coup is a battle of will, not strength, and the wolf struck the telling blow. Coming from behind, she tore a neat tuft of fur from the bear's haunch, and his growl swelled to a bellow. He spun around, hurt more in his pride than his flesh, but Marta was on the offensive. She snapped from the left and barked from the right. She ran head on toward his chest, then dodged away at the last second. Wild-eyed, she teased and tore at him in a frenzy. The bear lurched and snapped at her, but she only sheared closer, teeth clicking a hair's breadth from his hide. He made to rear up again, but the wolf took aim at his belly and he quickly dropped to all fours.

He paused for a moment, coolly, as Marta continued her furious assault. For now, the bear would have no

peace here. He glared at the blur of black whirling between him and the deer carcass. He growled tersely in
Marta's direction, turned with a snort, and ambled off.

Marta dove for the meat. She sank her teeth into the
deer with new relish and, casting a satisfied look in the
bear's direction, she ate until she could eat no more.

Meat drunk for the first time in weeks, her head
reeled as blood rushed to her stomach. She would need
water soon, but for now she pulled herself away from the
carcass and lay, half-panting, as the evening light fell
over the mountain. She rested until dark, then rolled to
her feet, sides bulging, and found her way back to the
hiker trail.

As she trotted down the sometimes-rocky path, her
feet hit the ground with new weight. Wherever this land
was, it would feed her. For now, its trails would be her
home.

THIRTY-THREE

gray wolf

The summit of Gray Wolf Mountain is not a cozy place. One of a dozen stony teeth at the western lip of the Mission Mountains, the peak rises into thin, cold air. On the day when Marta found herself at the foot of Gray Wolf Lake, looking up, the summit was hidden in the first blast of a late autumn blizzard.

Marta was strong again. Well fleshed from weeks of good hunting, her chest healed, a coat of winter fur now thickened across her chest and shoulders. Her body had recovered after her feast on the bear's buck, much as her spirit had recovered after her long sleep and dream. A lone wolf again, she fell easily into those ways. Once her strength returned, she had no need to scavenge meat or settle for small game; she tracked and killed deer and elk on her own.

The autumn urge to travel was strong, and for the past month it had pulled her through the Mission Mountains to the west, the Swan Mountains to the northeast, and the valley in between. She loped down logging roads, picked her way along ridgelines, and scrambled through brushy clearcuts. As hunting season brought more human traffic to the area, she kept to high places like this cirque.

Now she stood below Gray Wolf Glacier, light flakes falling from the blizzard above. All day, something had been pulling her up this slope. The trail was solitary, for one thing; no hunters got this far from the road. For another, she had never been here and had no picture of the land that lay on the other side of the pass.

Her feet tingled as she stood on the shore of the lake, looking toward the glacier. Clouds boiled over the ridge, and from above Marta heard an occasional clatter of stones, partly muffled by snow. The traveling urge was strong, but a cold smell in the air was stronger. This storm carried the weight of winter on its back.

If she stayed much longer, the flakes now falling in a cape around her shoulders would cover the ground. It would reach her knees, making traveling difficult; much higher, and traveling would be impossible. She could be swallowed in a tree well and suffocate or freeze to death. For this season, Gray Wolf Pass would have to wait.

Marta took a long look at the high country. As she looked, a curve of wind swirled down the cirque, sweeping past her in a flurry, and she lifted her head to answer. The wolf howl joined the first howl of winter.

Marta sang as the snow coated her ruff and the ridge of her back, icing her black silhouette in a layer of white. Flakes crusted her eyelashes and stuck to her whiskers, and she continued to sing. She sang into her own echo, changing tones as the sound came back from across the lake. An arc of winter wind merged with an arc of winter song, and as the echoes played into one another, it almost sounded like she was howling with her pack.

Marta stood for a moment, then shook bravely, spattering flakes into the whitening landscape, as one last arc of wind groaned after her. By dark, snow had covered the single line of wolf prints threading downward through the forest.

THIRTY-FOUR

hunting the hunted

Driven from the high places by weather, Marta spent the first weeks of winter hunting and trying not to be hunted. People with guns traveled the back roads at all times of day, and sometimes night. Marta continued exploring, using the roads when she could and the trails when she could not, making long-distance loops across the southern Swan Valley.

Throughout her travels Marta remained, as was her wont, unseen. Weeks in the busy Flathead Valley had made her an expert in elusion. She saw, but did not let herself be seen. She kept to the edges wherever she went, a shadow that never traced the same path twice. One moment she was a glimpse by the rocky Swan River, another, a dot on a hillside; one moment a shape behind a tree and the next, another piece in the jigsaw puzzle of night.

Though rarely seen, she was sometimes heard. From ridge tops and valleys, at full moon and new, came a song that had not been sung here for years. The deer heard, and the hide prickled on their backs. The lowland elk and moose heard, and swung their great racks high in surprise. Lions heard, and swished their long tails. Bobcats heard, and crouched warily at the sound. Coyotes heard, and sometimes sang back, a yodel skating high above Marta's chestier tones. When dogs heard they panicked, setting off a storm of barking. Few humans heard, except hunters and wood gatherers; those who did paused to listen to her song, and touched their chins in wonder.

Autumn had ended in a rush, and it was time for Marta to find a wintering ground. With no pack, she needed the best possible habitat: a place with running water, game, and shelter from the weather; a place where she could press hunting circuits into the snow; a place without much competition. Coyotes were all right to sing with, but Marta didn't need them scaring off her prey.

As Marta hunted for her meals, she hunted for a winter home. She tried the far side of Swan Lake, but was startled from her bed by early-morning fishermen.

She tried Bond Creek, but the creek bottom was too tangled; she preferred a mix of meadows and forest. On several small lakes that dotted the center of the valley, Marta found the summer homes deserted, but the human presence was still strong. Farther south, Salmon Lake had one huge house on a tiny island, and even it seemed abandoned—but the meadows there were too swampy and close to the road.

The road was the Swan Highway, a two-lane bar of asphalt that split the valley from north to south. Here the highway paralleled the Continental Divide, which ran wild and unbroken by roads for more than a hundred miles. Vehicles needing to cross that crest drove up or down the Swan, and the traffic was fast and unpredictable. No longer desperate enough to hunt bones from its ditches, Marta kept away from the highway.

In the last days of hunting season, Marta ranged cautiously through the foothills, searching for a winter home. Months had passed, and many sights and smells had filled her head since leaving Pleasant Valley. Nothing reminded her of it here. Now her hunt for home was not for a place she knew, but for a place where she could survive the deadliest season of the year. To find such a place, she had nothing but her own sense of direction. As her tracks through the Swan Valley showed, that pointed a different way every day.

Marta was exploring the foothills of the Mission Mountains, north and east of Gray Wolf, on the day she saw the deer fall over. It was a cold spell: record-breaking cold for humans and keep-moving weather for wolves. Marta had been on the move for a week, rarely stopping in her quest to keep warm and fed. That day she was running a logging road in the west Swan, on ruts packed hard by the loud machines that hunters sometimes rode through the snow. To stay alive in such weather, Marta had to hunt and eat often; earlier, in the hard air of that afternoon, she had picked up a promising scent on the road and had been pursuing it ever since.

The track was of a whitetail buck, big enough to feed Marta through the longest cold snap. His trail wove on and off the road, and where it went, Marta followed. The road passed among gentle ridges, some clear-cut and open for running, others well forested for shelter. A good feeling crept into Marta's paws as she trotted across the crusty snow, and it wasn't the cold. It was the land.

Marta's step was strong as she tracked the buck, drinking where it had drunk and resting where it had rested. Under a crackling sun, Marta's shape made a blue shadow on the bright snow, and ice gathered on her muzzle and ears. She heard snow machines far off, but gave them only a flick of the ear. She could disappear if the need arose.

Gradually she closed the distance on the buck. His sign grew fresher on the road, and the pulse in Marta's chest grew warmer. She paused here and there to listen for a snort of his icy breath, but all she heard was the creak of frozen tree limbs and the distant drone of the snow machines.

The machines kept their distance, and Marta pushed on. The closer she got to the buck, the stronger the feeling grew in her stomach. Finally she glimpsed the gray-brown of its winter coat, and gave chase. The buck heard the scrape of her step and without turning to look, bolted down the road. Marta matched his pace for a quarter mile, then lost ground. She slowed to a lope, and the buck did likewise. Then she sprinted again, and he pushed ahead still farther. When Marta gave chase a third time, the buck did not stop for nearly a mile; puffing steam and blinking back ice, Marta gave up. This deer had passed the wolf test and, as often happened, it was not worth her effort to continue.

For a while she followed the deer at a distance, neither tracking nor ignoring him. Thirsty, she dropped off the road at a gurgling creek and broke a hole in the ice. Between drinks, she saw the buck trot ahead as the whine of snowmobiles grew noisier. Without warning, one of the sounds zoomed to a stop not far ahead of her. The buck froze. Marta looked up, staring, as water droplets crystallized on her chin. The deer fell over. One moment he was standing motionless, snorting puffs of steam, and the next he simply fell over sideways. Marta closed her mouth in surprise, and the briefest instant later, the crack of a bullet clapped in her ears.

Other shots broke the air, cracking like ice, and human shouts sang out into the dense, bright afternoon. Minutes before, the buck had eluded Marta's best chase; now he had simply fallen in his tracks. His body jerked several times, followed by more cracks in the air. A taste rose in Marta's mouth, and her nose angled toward the smell of new blood. But her chest turned the other direction, away from the road. She followed her body, trotting beside the muted gurgle of the creek, deeper into the shelter of the trees. She would find her meal elsewhere.

THIRTY-FIVE

lindbergh lake

Marta found her meal, and she did not have to travel far. She sacked a young of the year doe not far down the creek and ate heartily, steam rising from the carcass. She ate fast; in this cold, the meat would be frozen by morning. She ate till she hurt; there was no way to know when or where she would find her next meal. Marta sniffed appreciatively at the remains, then rested until the cold woke her.

She went on exploring, following her feet. Just before nightfall she discovered Lindbergh Lake, a huge arm of water that elbowed its way through the ridges of the lower Missions. Covered in ice and snow, the lake was the perfect winter highway for a wolf—and for the prey she sought.

The good feeling in Marta's paws grew stronger as

she toured the ridges above the lake. The only tracks here were from wildlife; no snow machines came this way. The slopes were untraveled, and most of the streams ran free of ice. The deer were abundant, which would mean a hard winter for them but good hunting for Marta.

The days grew shorter, and after the intense cold let up, Marta found herself lingering in the area of Lindbergh Lake. It had the right combination of ridges and flats, thickets and clearings, running water and—most important—a boundless food supply. Shortly after she arrived, the whine of snowmobiles increased sharply for a day, then disappeared altogether. Marta had the hunting to herself.

Human hunters gone, Marta was at the top of the food chain. The bears were asleep for the season, and the few lions kept to themselves. Marta's prey was easy to find. In the lowlands was a network of deer yards, winter gathering places where herds banded together for safety and warmth. Between the yards and the brushy places where they browsed, the deer's hooves had worn good paths into the snow. This was a boon for Marta, now that she had no pack members to help break trail. The snowdrifts were coming chest high.

As the shortest day of the year approached, Marta picked out a system of trails between the deer yards and found places for resting and hiding. She had a lookout over the lake and knew shortcuts to and from open water. She was as well fed as a wolf could be, hunting alone in the middle of winter, which meant she skirted hunger constantly. When the turn of season finally came, that first extra moment of daylight, she was still healthy: she had no injuries, no sore spots, no wheeze in her breath or dimming in her eyes. That was good. Being strong in the middle of winter was a sign that she might survive until spring.

Not long after the turn of day, Marta made a startling discovery. At the eastern border of her hunting territory, she found a set of strange tracks. Wolf tracks! Marta had not seen the sign of another wolf since she left Nyack Creek. Here and there she had seen old marks, mostly in the deeper wilderness, but nothing recent—not within a year. These tracks, when she found them in fresh snow, had been made within the last day. They were huge. At first they didn't seem like wolf, they were so big; the animal they belonged to could be twice Marta's size. As an enemy or even a competitor, such a creature would be dangerous. Fortunately, whoever this strange wolf was, it had not touched her territory. He— the scent marks were definitely male—had come as far as her own marks, but not crossed the line.

Marta planted her hind feet and marked the

stranger's tracks with a furious stream. Then she cut loose with a howl. Stronger than any song she had sung in weeks, her voice resonated across the land. She sang "I was here first" and "this is my territory," and ended each song on a clear warning note. Then she squatted again and marked her own sign decisively over his. NO TRESPASSING, the sign read.

Marta spent the rest of that day checking her territory. She did not hunt, though she was hungry; instead, she marked each of the scent posts that defined her hunting ground. It took until after nightfall, and she'd started at midday; she had nearly ten miles to cover, and the winter light made for a short day. She completed her task in the early hours of darkness, watched over by the half-carved orb of a crescent moon.

When Marta finally reached her bed on the ridge, she was exhausted. Too tired to hunt and nearly too tired to eat, she dug up a small cache of food. Choosing a leg from one of her kills, she gnawed wearily at the frozen muscle and hide. She fought sleep until she had eaten all the way to the bone, then dozed in the snow.

When she awoke the moon was down, and she had only the stars for company. Still tired from too much work and too little food, Marta did not stir from her bed. She lifted her head and lay quietly, listening to the lake below. The ice was shifting. A new crack announced itself with a hiss, and a plate of ice responded with a re-sounding boom. The tremor set off another crack, and a high-pitched whine sang straight down the middle of the lake. Marta listened drowsily, secure in her snow bed, as the ice made a symphony against the night.

Then suddenly, a different melody soared above the lake. Above the ice music Marta heard one plaintive, elegant wolf call rising from the ridge on the south side of the lake. She shook the sleep from her head. This call was for her.

It was the song of a traveler, a lone wolf announcing his presence, and Marta listened intently. This would be the visitor whose tracks she had seen, and his song might tell if he was staying or going, friend or enemy. In the dull scatter of light from the sky, only the tips of her ears moved as she bent toward the sound. Her nose twitched furiously, as if she could smell all the way across the lake. But the song, when it was done, answered no questions. It was just wolf music, which Marta had not heard in months, and it warmed her throat.

Something pulled Marta to her feet. It pulled like a string from the tip of her nose all the way to her tail, pulled her upright in one fluid motion, aligned her bones and closed her eyes and opened her jaws and, oh, the song she sang. It was a star song and a lake song and a song of plenty; a song of good wintering grounds and long, healthy nights, a song of the strong feeling in her paws. A song of wolf ways. A song of survival. Marta sang, and stopped. No call returned across the frozen lake.

All was still again, and Marta sniffed at her mostly eaten leg bone. The silence of the strange wolf, whoever he was, meant one thing: for now, he posed no threat. Marta pawed her bone close, lay down, and pulled the marrow end toward her. For a long time she lay absorbed with it, drawing out the rich center with her teeth and tongue. When she was finished she curled in the snow and slept, deep and dreamless, until morning.

THIRTY-SIX

solitude

Snow came again in a few days, covering the strange wolf's tracks. No new tracks appeared, and Marta was again the only wolf in her winter range. There was never a lack of deer to hunt, though some were harder to catch than others. Some weeks she went hungrier, other weeks fuller. Through it she stayed warm at night, and her muscles barely burned when she ran. Her fur was bright and her nose moist. She remained without a pack for companionship, but at Lindbergh Lake she was never entirely alone.

Marta came to know the other winter residents of the drainage. She learned the habits of the different deer herds, the elk, and the moose that lived nearby. She kept an eye on the rabbits, otter, and beaver, too, but more for interest than food; deer kept her well fed.

As for competitors, there was one lion in the area, but her territory barely overlapped with Marta's. Bobcats kept small game on the run and couldn't really compete for large animals. Marta grew accustomed to the hoarse shriek of the lynx, and it became a natural part of the winter night. Coyotes sometimes dug into her food caches or cleaned up a kill before Marta was done, but were only a nuisance, never a danger. There was plenty of hunting to go around.

In one part of the lowlands, Marta had the company of a pair of red foxes. Sometimes she would stop to rest nearby, just out of sight, and watch them hunting their part of the food chain. Another time she might see them playing tag as she and Calef once had done. The foxes' tails swept magically through the air, flowing behind them as they darted under and around the stumpy brush of the old logging areas. Healthy and in the prime of life, like Marta they had found Lindbergh Lake a good place to survive the hardest season of the year.

Of all the animals, Marta was closest to the ravens. Throughout her life, she had kept company with one or more of these big, talkative birds. Raven and wolf were unofficial allies in the forest; they listened for each other's calls and led one another to kills. Just as the ravens had helped Marta, she helped them. If the birds seemed hungrier than usual, she might leave extra scraps of meat on a carcass, and if the birds pecked at it while she was chewing on a separate bone, she did not chase them away.

Marta was closest to the ravens, but she knew the deer best. They were her livelihood, and she studied them closely. Along her snow-packed hunting circuits, she came to know their tracks and scents as well as their different pairings and groupings. Some individuals she picked out as potential meals, and others she admired for their speed or grace. That winter, there was one animal she watched for yet another reason. It was an old buck, a leader of one of the herds.

As soon as she arrived in the area, Marta had noticed his scent. She could always pick it out from others on the trail. Something was special about him: not just the regal tilt of his shoulders or the authority in his voice; not just the graceful way he carried his antlers through the firs or the way other deer looked at him. The buck was a survivor. He had lived to an old age, leading his band through many seasons. Though the old deer was pitifully slow on his feet, it never occurred to Marta to chase him. This buck was not food.

In the company of these and others, the black wolf wintered peacefully in the shadow of the Mission Mountains. The days grew longer, and ice melted from the streambeds. Snow dissolved on the surface of the lake and sometimes fell from the sky warm and mixed with rain. These days, Marta's fox neighbors held their tails higher when they played. The deer traveled more and rested less, seeking out hidden patches of browse to take them through the last bony days of winter.

As the weather warmed, the snow trails turned to slush and the deer yards grew muddy. While the world melted outside, something began to soften and flow inside Marta, too. The ground warmed under the pads of her paws, sending a twinge up her forelegs. The itch was setting in: the itch to travel, to move, to run with the season. But it was not yet time to leave the safety of her winter range. The does were barely showing the weight of their young, and late blizzards still passed through the mountains.

On a calm evening toward the end of winter, Marta stood on the ridge overlooking Lindbergh Lake. The afternoon dimmed, blurring the gray network of cracks in the lake ice. There was no wind, and no other sound except the hop of a rabbit across the snow. Marta had had a good week of hunting and paid no attention to the hopping. She surveyed the ridge beyond the lake, and the ridges beyond it to the south. Soon—as soon as the weather allowed—she would be running over them.

And in that moment of calm, there came another kind of noise that would change everything. From beyond the lake, many ridges to the south, rose a song: a wolf song. Marta had heard this voice before. It was the strange wolf, the male who had come and gone a few weeks earlier, the male whose tracks were twice the size of hers. Greatfoot was back.

THIRTY-SEVEN

greatfoot

Greatfoot's sign appeared the next day. Huge tracks dented the softening snow, and his scent marked trees along his trail. Marta took note of his movements, and as before, he kept a respectful distance. He was hunting nearby, including deer from within Marta's territory, but still did not cross the boundary she had set.

Marta did not actually see her neighbor for almost a week, and when she did, it was from afar. From her lake overlook she glanced down one morning and there he was, loping along the edge of the ice, hunting. Marta watched as he followed his prey's scent, tracking and backtracking in lines and loops. He kept an even pace, stopping only to sniff the air or prick his ears to sounds Marta could not hear. When he disappeared around the elbow in the lake, she rose and picked her way along the ridge, tracing his progress.

Greatfoot was tireless. He followed the shore steadily, diving in and out of the woods, and Marta followed from above. She was following him to protect the western side of her hunting grounds, but she was also curious. This wolf had a certain lilt to his pace, a quality that kept her attention. She watched his progress for hours.

He seemed to hunt for the joy of it, not just from hunger. Where other wolves hunted efficiently, he hunted extravagantly: he ran deep into the woods when running shallow would do; he ran fast when slow would do, far when near would do. He had a huge stride to match his huge feet, and even Marta—now as strong as she had ever been—had to rest from following him. That this was a wolf of endurance was obvious, even from a mile away and hundreds of feet up.

Greatfoot made his kill far down the lake from where he had started. Marta did not see it; she only saw him veer off the shore and into the woods on a test chase. She sat, catching her breath, and he did not veer back out of the woods. Her breath had settled when she heard a wolf howl: a killing howl. Marta had watched his hunt with such intensity that she found herself howling in response. A moment later, when her stomach juices started to flow, she clapped her fine jaws shut. What was she singing about? There was no food in front of her.

Marta stood, but Greatfoot had heard her short echo from across the lake, and his song took on a new note. Marta barked gruffly in the direction of her western boundary, then turned and trotted back down the ridge. She had hunting of her own to do.

For the next week Greatfoot remained at large on Lindbergh, but Marta paid little heed. The season was shifting faster now. As the daily light was growing, so was her urge to travel, and Marta began to drift from her territory, taking long loops out beyond the easy paths. She crossed trails with Greatfoot occasionally, trading scent marks, but never met him directly.

One day when Marta was returning home, she noticed Greatfoot's unmistakable footprint in the softening snow. He was barely ahead of her, and his print was a hunting print. Marta's back went up; he was headed straight for her deer herd. There were deer to spare, but the way of the wolf was to share hunting only with one's pack—and Marta had no pack.

Her back went up, and so did her speed. She sprinted until she heard Greatfoot's step in the snow, then dropped back and kept pace. She was not eager to face a wolf whose paw print covered nearly two of hers. As she followed, she discovered he was indeed hunting—hunting her home herd. Marta knew all their scents now, and she smelled her old favorite, the lead buck, in the tracks.

Suddenly she heard a grunt and a feathery sound in the snow ahead. Greatfoot had taken to chase, testing one of the animals. In the same instant she heard a snort, and something heaved in her chest: it was the great buck. Greatfoot was testing him.

Marta's response was instantaneous. She plunged forward, eyes electric and black ruff standing out in spikes, and ran reckless after both wolf and prey. She had little time in which to catch them. Marta surged ahead and soon could taste the spray of slush from Greatfoot's back feet. He did not hear her; he only heard and saw the old buck.

The other deer had scattered into the woods, and their leader was achingly slow. It was no contest between wolf and deer. Greatfoot was just four lengths from the buck, one big-footed lunge away, when a fearful bellow came from behind and a silver-black force spun into his field of vision. Marta.

The first thing he saw was her teeth. The roaring shape took focus in front of Greatfoot's face, and with a mighty snap, Marta's jaws closed a breath away from Greatfoot's throat. In the instant before she roared again, half howl and half growl, he skidded to a stop and spread his own jaws in her direction.

Marta ducked and rolled out of reach, then came to her feet barking. This was her territory, her winter home. These herds were her lifeline and this, more than any other, was her buck. Greatfoot barked back, a booming response. They were barely inside Marta's territory. Until that moment, the old buck had been Greatfoot's chase.

The two barked back and forth, ruffs filled out, backs up, circling furiously. Each growled low, waiting for the other to attack. Marta barked and Greatfoot barked; Marta circled and Greatfoot circled. They barked and circled until their voices cracked. Finally Greatfoot paused. He was on Marta's turf, and despite his size, she was not backing down. When he paused, Marta paused; the barking slowed. The growls lessened. The silence grew.

Their clamor all but over, Marta made a final move— a token snap, to confirm her claim—at Greatfoot's nose. He yipped sharply and lifted a huge paw, but Marta's eye stopped him.

He put his paw back on the ground. Silence. He sniffed, nostrils barely moving. Then Marta barked, but it was not the same bark as before. Greatfoot sniffed again. Marta barked again in the new way—and then she, too, sniffed. Greatfoot opened his mouth as if to bark back, but his voice came out a low cry that lengthened into a howl. Marta's eyes deepened, and the shape of her fur changed around her face. Her ears softened. She stepped forward and sniffed quizzically at his muzzle. Then she barked again, but the end of her voice trailed out and rose into a call that curved all the way up into the afternoon sky. Greatfoot rounded his lips into another howl, and wound his song around hers.

Not far away in the trees, a single pair of ears flicked back and forth at the sound. The old buck let out a gust of air through his nostrils and stalked loudly away, but neither wolf heard.

Marta had met her match.

THIRTY-EIGHT

running together

Strange wolves did not always get along well, as Marta had learned long ago. After her run-in with the black wolf years before, she avoided strangers. The way of the wolf, except among pack members, was to keep one's distance. Any contact was a risk, and when contact was made, it meant there was a conflict to settle or an advantage to be gained.

Finding packmates was a delicate process. The pack was much more than a casual group of loners who came and went; it was a family. To get along in a family that hunted together, traveled together, and even shared food, all the members had to cooperate and communicate. That took time, and it took a blend of strength and style that didn't come together just by chance. Members were usually born and raised into a pack, not added as adults;

even wolves related by blood didn't always take to one another, as Marta knew from her birth pack. For strange wolves to form a pack took unusual circumstances, unusual luck, or both.

By the time they met face-to-face, Marta and Greatfoot were not quite strangers. For weeks before the standoff over the buck, they had studied each other as they crossed paths around Lindbergh Lake. Neither had challenged the other and both had plenty to eat, so there was little cause for conflict. When their confrontation finally came, it didn't last.

That Marta and Greatfoot were each ending the winter alone, the only wolves for hundreds of miles, was an unusual circumstance. That their scents were right and their signals matched was luck. Standing together in the soft snow of the clearing, the buck forgotten, each wolf turned full attention on the other.

Greatfoot sniffed gingerly at Marta's muzzle, then at her collar. Marta held still for a moment, then sniffed back. As she did, the wrinkles softened in Greatfoot's forehead, and his ears went back. Cautiously they sniffed closer, alert to the tiniest changes of breath and stance. Neither wolf tried to dominate as the two explored the space between them, and Marta's tail slowly lost its angry bent. When their eyes finally met, no sign of threat remained in either face. Greatfoot did not turn to leave Marta's territory, and she did not chase him away.

In the next days, the wolves followed one another's every move. Closer and closer they came, observing in detail what they had sensed at a distance. When Marta made the play face, Greatfoot's ears went forward in kind; when she made the warning face, his ears went back. The two began running together. Running led to playing and playing to hunting; eating together led to exploring together, and soon their tracks made a single line through the coarse, grainy snow.

The wolves' urge to travel grew, and every day they ventured farther from Marta's winter home. In the week when buds began to swell on the huckleberry bushes, Marta and Greatfoot left Lindbergh Lake for good.

They ran south along thawing roads into the Jocko River drainage. The Jocko was quiet this time of year. Logging trucks were idle, and snow machines had abandoned the muddy trails. Marta and Greatfoot had the forest to themselves: they had the mountains, the timber, the clear-cuts, their choice of deer and elk, and only the flat, fast-running river for company.

Marta and Greatfoot followed the Jocko west until it ran into the lower Flathead Valley. Fences and roads circled every meadow, and houses dotted the ranch land as they did in the upper Flathead, where Marta had last dodged civilization. She and Greatfoot dodged it again, retracing their steps back into the forest.

As the days grew longer, the urge to run broke free from its winter cage, and the wolves ran the valleys and ridges of the Missions and Swans as wolves had done in ancient times. They ran like fire galloping up a mountainside; they ran like streams roaring under a snow bridge. They hunted with new hunger and played like youngsters. Shoots of green took hold underneath the snow as they ran, and over their heads the sun rose higher and higher, as if to grasp and shake out the blanket of white that had lain over the high country all winter.

The Jocko did not hold them for long; now that spring was coming, nothing could. In the next weeks, Marta and Greatfoot headed in every direction: a little south, a little east, some north, back south, west, and south again. They followed the wolf compass wherever their noses pointed, discovering the long valleys west of the great divide: Jocko, Rattlesnake, and Blackfoot; Monture, Rattlesnake, Ovando, Ninemile, and Rattlesnake again.

The wolves explored old timber, abandoned trails, and softening river bottoms, hunting and playing as wolf packs had done centuries before. Most of those packs were larger than two, but when it came to survival, the difference between one wolf and two was difference enough. Marta and Greatfoot became a pack.

THIRTY-NINE

rock creek

Even the widest swath of forest was hardly wide enough for a pair of healthy wolves on the move. On a day when the snow crusted over and running was easy, Marta and Greatfoot could cross half a mountain range, hunt and kill a meal, feast and nap, and be off the mountain before dark—with time for games and grooming in between. On days they didn't hunt, they could travel farther or play more.

The back country was their own for now, but few of the forests were more than a day wide. Where the woods ran out, the wolves ran into people: their highways, houses, animals, and their scents of metal and oil. For the most part, Marta and Greatfoot left the human places to the humans. When they did go near, it was often at night and out of necessity—to get from one forest to the next—and rarely from curiosity.

After leaving the Jocko Valley, Marta and Greatfoot spent days exploring the Rattlesnake Wilderness. South of the wilderness ran a freeway: not a two-lane highway like the Swan but a four-lane interstate. One cool morning, they reached the freeway at Rock Creek. Cars and trucks hurtled past, pushing gusts of wind over the wolves' backs as they waited below the rise of the road. Grit peppered their faces. Greatfoot seemed to have no fear, but Marta was edgy; she still cringed at the possibility of being seen.

At the first break in traffic, the wolves dashed across the highway. On Rock Creek they found a road little used by human beings, but well traveled by many other animals. Marta and Greatfoot were hungry enough to chase test a deer, but by now winter had taken the weakest of the herds, and the wolves were not yet hungry enough for more than easy hunting.

The sun warm on their backs, Greatfoot and Marta continued lazily up the drainage. They played tag on the snow-packed road and stopped to drink from the swollen creek. Moose tracks ambled in and out of the brush, but the wolves barely noticed. Today other things were more interesting, like the bounce and splash of the river, the taste of greening grass, and smells rising from the melting snow. Marta, in addition, was noticing a different kind of spring energy, the kind that came from inside: her breeding time was coming.

As the day bloomed around them, Marta's games of tag became more pointed and her pace more reckless. She ran up hills and down again, circling in on Greatfoot with a hummingbird's precision. On one downhill run, thundering straight for the creek, she sideswiped his flank with a playful nip. He lunged at her but missed, hanging his head as Marta sailed over the bank and made a solid four-foot landing in the water. Planting her feet in the icy rapids, she turned to face him, gulping mouthfuls of bubbles from the torrent and shooting defiant looks in his direction.

Wrinkles appeared in the dark markings above Greatfoot's eyes. If he jumped in, she would jump out; if he stayed out, she would stay in. His ears flicked forward and back as he paced the creek bank, keeping an eye on Marta's mischief. In midstep he caught scent of a tantalizing track. He stopped, pressing his nose to the earth, and discovered a second, smaller track. Two fresh tracks made that morning. Moose tracks. Greatfoot's play face changed suddenly to the hunting face, and he whined faintly. His pace widened into a run, dodging back and forth as he investigated the tracks. They led across the creek.

Without a glance at Marta, Greatfoot gathered his legs and sprang past her. But at the last push of takeoff, his hind feet slipped on a wet boulder, and instead of soaring onto the other bank, he landed with a splash in the deepest part of the current. Marta saw the whitewater sweep him under. The mischief went out of her and she scrambled back to shore, barking when she saw two of his great paws beat the air and disappear again.

A few breaths later, his gray snout and drenched head reared up from the current. Snorting out a gust of water, Greatfoot righted himself as the swift current continued dragging him downstream. Then with a few strokes he paddled, still snorting, to the far shore. Pulling onto the bank he shook, coughed, and shook again. He looked back upstream until he found Marta, and their eyes locked. When he barked, it was a hunting bark. He put his nose to the ground and disappeared into a thicket of poplars.

Marta remained on her side of the creek. Standing in the whitewater to show off was one thing, but getting rolled in it was something else again. She didn't have Greatfoot's bulk to protect against underwater boulders or his strength to pull free of the current. What she did have was the spring blood, and it drew her toward Greatfoot. Instead of pulling her into the water, it pulled her back onto the road, and Marta raced downstream along the bank, eyeing the creek for a shallow or calm place in its rapids. Finally she saw a poplar trunk fallen across the stream. She trotted across it and sprinted back to the place where she had last seen Greatfoot.

His tracks followed the moose tracks, and she followed both into the poplars. The trail meandered from one swampy area to the next, a pattern of steps belonging to a cow moose and a smaller yearling. The cow's tracks pressed heavily into the mud; she was probably pregnant. The big wolf tracks looped this way and that, pursuing but not yet chasing the pair. Greatfoot, as usual, was taking the long way.

Suddenly Marta heard a great bellow. There was a crash, then the sound of slush spewing and branches breaking. Another bellow, and silence. Then several short, hoarse grunts, silence, and the thump of a hoof. There were no wolf sounds. Marta crept toward the noise until she saw what it meant: Greatfoot was backed against a clump of willows, flanked by a cow moose on one side and a smaller, mean-looking bull on the other. Both had murder in their eyes, and the mother had the size and hooves to do it. From her hiding place Marta could see that the cow wasn't pregnant. She was just enormous.

Marta watched, blood pounding, as the cow lowered her head toward Greatfoot. The gray wolf did not move, holding a steady gaze on her and her offspring. When the cow reared back to attack, Marta sprang from her crouch and charged. Aiming for the nearest moose flesh, she snapped at the rump of the yearling, but got only a mouthful of fur and a moment of his attention. As the bull whirled toward his attacker, the cow glanced too— just for an instant, but it was the instant Greatfoot needed. He dodged, and the cow's blunt hoof missed his skull, landing painfully on his foot. Wrenching free, the gray wolf shot out from the willows and into the woods. As Greatfoot darted in one direction, Marta darted in the other, leaving the moose pair with mayhem in their eyes and nowhere to aim it.

Marta heard Greatfoot running through the swamps and circled to follow. She still had a mouthful of fur and a taste for blood, but she did not look back. She wasn't half as hungry as the cow was mad, and as Marta streaked back toward Rock Creek, she could smell the swampy breath of the moose pumping into the air behind her tail.

Marta ran full speed, putting her footprints two by two into Greatfoot's larger ones. Her blood had been stirred up before the confrontation; now it was rolling like spring runoff. Panting, she chased after her partner, racing to catch up with him. A different kind of hunger was pulling her now.

FORTY

wolf love

Wolf love is sometimes slow and sometimes sudden. Between Greatfoot and Marta, what began slowly at Lindbergh Lake grew suddenly after the pair left Rock Creek. They crossed the freeway in darkness and traveled north, following game trails that led up the hills and into the forest. As they traveled, Marta's inner urge grew, and the breeding scent rose from her breath and fur. Greatfoot responded with a scent and an urge of his own, and the two touched often as they wound deeper into the night.

In the sanctuary of the Rattlesnake Wilderness, on a moonless night between winter and spring, one gray wolf and one black danced courtship in a dust of new snow. The last time wild wolves had courted in that canyon, there were no roads; no cars; no hum of airplane overhead; no sky glow from the city. Back then the human presence was slight, scattered in camps along the river. Now their boxy homes filled the lower canyon, and their smells were carried on every breeze.

Still, Marta and Greatfoot danced. It was the dance of the male and female done for millennia on this land, and it was back. They chased, they howled, they sprang over stumps and under limbs; they stood nose to nose, panting steam in the still, cool air. They nuzzled one another—sometimes gentle, sometimes wild—and the chase was on again.

Greatfoot rode up on Marta and Marta rode up on Greatfoot in the play written millions of years ago that still shone in their golden eyes. When the scent was right, they tied. The dark silver of one shape merged with the frosted black of the other, and they remained so for a long time. Long enough for a breeze to come up and make the tiniest tree branches wave happily against the sky. Long enough for the snow to soften under Marta's paws. Long enough for a late moon to rise and peer through the overcast. Long enough for the silver to mix with the black and for the race to go on. Long enough.

FORTY-ONE

evaro crossing

After Marta and Greatfoot mated, their travels took on a new urgency. They were a pair, and a pair needed a territory. Before long there could be wolf pups, and they would need a den site, good hunting, safe rendezvous sites, and room to roam without human interference. For Marta and Greatfoot, the hunt for home was on.

The Rattlesnake was not home. City glow tinged the sky at night, and jets shuddered overhead during the day. For a wilderness it was small, and the wild heart of the valley had been cut out. A road ran upstream, bringing cars and people to and from the houses that grew up around the creek.

The Swan Valley was not home either. It was big enough, a two-day run from north to south, but except for places like Lindbergh Lake in the middle of winter, people had claimed it as their own. The Blackfoot Valley was too narrow and the Clark Fork, though broad, was halved by the same freeway that ran past Rock Creek; while Greatfoot and Marta could cross it, they could not live on top of it.

When logging trucks returned to the back roads, Marta and Greatfoot retreated to the woods. The wolves tried to avoid people, but people were everywhere. Their homes fronted the forest, and their cars sped through it. When Marta and Greatfoot could not find a way around a human place, they passed by at the edges. Usually they went unnoticed, unless dogs were nearby.

Marta ignored pet dogs as she did other human things, but Greatfoot could not. A dog was strangely like a wolf in looks and smell, and strangely unlike in other ways. The way of the wolf was a strict code, and dogs didn't follow it. Only a few could howl at all, and their songs were without meaning: never a proper hunting howl, come-here howl or stay-away howl, just a confusing mixture of tones. Most dogs just stood and barked, the same noise over and over. Sometimes Greatfoot charged toward it and sometimes he ran away from it, but it always raised his hackles.

One day when travel was easy and their energy high, Marta and Greatfoot made a long run to the west, looping wide into the mountains around the northern outskirts of the city. On the last crust of snow, they slipped along the far side of the mountain, avoiding late season skiers, and headed for the top of Evaro Hill.

An ancient travel corridor for wildlife moving west and east, Evaro had also become a north-south corridor for humans traveling between the Missoula and Flathead valleys. Evaro Hill was long and steep. Downhill traffic rushed past in a blink, but uphill traffic was slow. Semi trucks crawled upward with much grinding of metal and fumes of oil, and smaller vehicles darted around them.

Nearing the highway from the trees, Marta and Greatfoot listened to the sounds, preparing to dash across at the first silence in the two streams of traffic. As they waited, Greatfoot grew restless. He chased a ground squirrel, followed an old elk track, then finally went to the fringe of the trees where he could see as well as hear the vehicles. Marta kept hidden. Suddenly she heard a frenzy of barking, an irritated clamor that included Greatfoot's voice.

She reached the edge of the trees in time to see Greatfoot standing on the shoulder of the highway as a pickup truck labored slowly past. His glare was fixed on two pet retrievers racing back and forth in the bed of the pickup, and all three animals were barking furiously.

Greatfoot was oblivious to the highway, ignoring both the rush of a down-bound car and the grind of a semi coming up. Marta waited until the car was safely out of sight, and before the truck came into view, she scrambled out of the trees.

Streaking past Greatfoot, she startled her mate with one short, sharp bark in his ear, and sped across the road. Greatfoot's reflex was to give chase, and before he knew it, both he and Marta were safely in the trees on the far side of the highway. Behind them in the uphill lane, the big semi rolled past the place where the gray wolf had been standing seconds before.

Greatfoot grabbed Marta's muzzle in his. She stood, chin high, as he applied a long lick to her face and neck. Then, still panting, Greatfoot looked down until his forehead barely touched her cheek. They stood that way for a moment, breath coming in short pulses as the sounds of the highway passed behind them. Marta whined then, a half breath that ended in a yip, and broke from their touch. She began running west, away from the highway, on the Evaro trail.

Greatfoot followed, and by dusk they were on the ridge above the Ninemile Valley. Marta and Greatfoot had been here when the snow was soft and deep, too deep for exploring, and they had gone no farther than the first creek.

The landscape looked different today, and not just because of the season. Today the wolves were looking for more than food; they were looking for home. From the top of Reservation Divide, Marta and Greatfoot could see the whole expanse of the Ninemile Valley. It was a gentle basin of a valley with more forests than clear-cuts on either side, and large checkerboards of pasture and trees in between.

The Ninemile was twice as big as Pleasant Valley, but at this time of year, the evening light slanted the same way over its length. As beams of sunlight broke through the clouds and played across the winter-green hills, the wolves saw what they were looking for. They saw hiding places in the trees, and creeks that ran year-round. They saw few roads and fewer houses.

Mostly they saw tracks. As at Lindbergh Lake, the deer were so abundant that they had carved deep travel routes between their winter yards and browsing places. From the ridge, Marta and Greatfoot saw more whitetail country than they could hunt in a lifetime. There were cattle, too, in the pastures below, but not enough to drive out the deer.

All was quiet that afternoon in the Ninemile, except for a single blue pickup truck driving slowly down the gravel road. As the light faded, a look came over Greatfoot's face and a song started in his throat. It was a hunting song, but not one Marta had heard before: a new hunting song for a new place. Marta joined in quickly—she was hungrier these days—and they chorused from the ridge as the sun played itself out into darkness. The wolves let their voices rise into the cooling air and were rewarded by a crash of hooves in the brush below them. With a flash of silver and black tails, Marta and Greatfoot bounded toward the noise.

The animal's scent hit both wolves at once, and both came to a halt. There was no deer in the brush, only a wayward steer. Neither wolf was hungry enough to see the gawky, strong-smelling creature as food, and they gave each other a short, disappointed howl. Leaving the terrified steer to lurch away through the underbrush, they trotted back uphill in search of real food.

It wasn't long before the wolves had their quarry. Marta made the first strike, pulling the doe off balance. She tottered and, as Greatfoot sprang forward, fell over. The wolves' jaws met at the throat and closed around it with one bite. The body wrenched, and Marta took a violent kick to her hindquarters. A twinge shot up her spine, but she held on; at least the hoof had not connected with her belly, where tiny life was just beginning to form.

The wolf pair fed well. Marta finished first, pulling away from the carcass to lie down. Cleaning herself in the darkness, she heard more than saw Greatfoot continue feeding until he, too, was full. He went to Marta, who rose, sniffing him appreciatively. One lick became two, and a nip became a hearty wolf kiss with much wagging of tails. Drowsy then, bellies slung low, they lumbered toward the nearest creek for a long drink. Soon the two were settled for the night. They curled up as far as their bloated bellies would allow and slept the sleep of the satisfied.

FORTY-TWO

den hunting

Marta and Greatfoot settled in the Ninemile. It held a few more people and cattle than Pleasant Valley, but it was much larger: wide enough for the people and cows to spread out on the valley floor and long enough for wolves to pass through unseen.

Separately and together, Marta and Greatfoot set the boundaries of their territory and marked scent trails within it. Scouting cautiously, the wolves found secret corridors that linked wildland to wildland, and they explored the wide bands of mountain and forest that surrounded the valley. Greatfoot discovered a favorite corridor to the west, and often crossed the freeway for long, exuberant hunts in the Lolo Forest and nearby Idaho.

Greatfoot's long hunts were not for lack of closer

game. The Ninemile danced with prey. Whitetail sprang from the unlikeliest places at every time of day; they seemed to be hiding behind every stump in the woods and every clump of grass in the pasture. Food was so plentiful that the wolves often cached their kill, burying the leftovers for later.

There was little competition for the prey. At first, a coyote pack from Reservation Divide came down to raid the caches, but after a close call with Greatfoot, they stayed away from the marked wolf territory. Bears, for the most part, liked higher places with more huckleberries. Except for a mountain lion who sneaked down from Siegel Creek from time to time—a long walk for a secretive animal—Marta and Greatfoot had the big hunting to themselves.

The wolves were used to staying out of sight and posed little trouble for the ranchers, but dogs were a problem. Pets and working dogs ran everywhere, confusing the wolves' careful scent marks and cluttering the air with random sounds. They irritated Greatfoot to the point of recklessness, and once he chased a dog all the way to its front porch in daylight. In every other way, the wolves fit into the valley as if they had always lived there. Despite new wolf tracks in the mud, wolf song in the air, and a wolf-killed deer every few days, life in the Ninemile went on as before.

Winter wound down slowly at first, and as it did, Marta became more aware of the life growing inside her. First a tightness across her belly and later a fullness in her womb were unmistakable. She was pregnant. In a few weeks, their pack of two would become a pack of more; how many more was impossible to tell. This time, at least, she would have Greatfoot's help feeding them.

The alpha urge grew in Marta along with the coming litter. Her will to live expanded once more, and her own survival was no longer enough; survival included the life of her mate and, most important, her unborn pups. The alpha instinct rose in Greatfoot too, and he grew protective. These days he was quick to the kill when they hunted and quick to stand between Marta and danger.

Soon Marta began hunting for a home within a home, a safe den site where they would raise the new pups. The Ninemile was riddled with clear-cuts and roads, which made travel and hunting easy for wolves, but also made it hard to find a place safe from intruders. Marta confined her search to the south-facing hills, where there was more sunlight and less logging than on the other side of the valley.

As the last pockets of snow hardened into cakes, Marta took her search to Kennedy Creek. Her paws were sore from the crusty ground and from the new weight in her belly, but she kept on. Time was growing short. Digging out a den was no small task, and her energy was already beginning to flag. By midday she reached the source of the creek, almost at the crest of the divide, and still had not found what she was looking for. She quenched her thirst at the stream, rested, then turned around to try again.

Instead of going down the snow-pocked way she had come up, Marta found her way onto a dirt road. Picking her way around the sharper stones and melting shards of ice, she did not hear the sound of a car engine idling out of sight on the road. She did not hear the engine shut off or the car door click open and shut. She heard only the tick of her toenails on the road and the breath pushing in and out of her mouth as she trotted downhill, nose to the ground.

The shot caught Marta off guard. At the first crack from the rifle her head swung up, a mistake that brought the buzz of the bullet that much closer to her skull. It missed, and she dodged toward the ditch on her right— where the second bullet buried itself in the snow underneath her. She dodged left then, flying over the road to the opposite ditch. Two more shots whistled by, and instead of ducking for cover she leaped upward, shooting an arc over the embankment. She didn't clear it. Crashing chest first into the top of the slope, she scrambled over as another bullet plowed into the mud a long step above her nose. This time Marta did not flinch, dodge, or change course. She simply placed her legs over the bullet hole in the earth and pushed upward with all her strength.

The final bullet was aimed not at Marta, but at the sky. The sound of a voice exploded in the air as Marta lay flat, panting. The snow was cold on her tight belly. She froze in that position, hearing a door open and close, and did not move. She heard an engine start and a car drive slowly away. Still she did not move. She listened, heart pounding, as an ordinary silence returned to the woods. When a screech sounded overhead she nearly stopped breathing—but it was only a blue-crested jay. No cars came, and still Marta did not move. By the time she shifted a stiff leg, preparing to get up, her warmth had melted a long trough in the snow.

By then, something else had happened. In the stillness Marta had felt the first quickening in her womb. Something stirred, the barest flutter of life swimming inside her. If she had not been motionless for so long, she would have missed it. In the wet snow, the wolf gazed back at her belly and cocked her head slightly, as if listening.

Then she stood, shook herself more gently than she might have, and skidded carefully back down the embankment.

FORTY-THREE

discovery

Later that day, Marta found a place to start digging. The soil was firm, painfully so. Still sore from icy paths, her paws curled hard as she scraped out the clay. She dug and scraped, dug and scraped, stopping only to clean the muck from her claws.

When she had made a head-size hole in the hillside, she stopped to rest. The smells were good here, and the creek gurgled nearby. No human sounds rose from the valley below, and the forest sounds were peaceful. Marta rested, licking her forefeet and nodding toward sleep. Suddenly she jerked awake, and her eyes swiveled around to her belly. Marta cocked her head: there it was again, the swimming. She stared at the taut skin of her underside, but the motion did not come again. Before her eyes could droop back toward sleep, they went wide and her ears went forward. Another vehicle was coming up the road.

Marta fled. She didn't notice that the sound of this engine was different from the other, that it was a deeper, cleaner rumble, or that it moved more slowly up the road. It was a motor, and the last one Marta had heard brought gunshots.

She bounded through the thick woods, transformed from a sleepy mother-to-be into a four-legged athlete. She leaped over stumps, ducked under leaning timber, and sidestepped new trees. Sore paws forgotten, she did not take the road. She took anything but the road and kept running until the noise faded to nothing behind her.

Marta was well into the next creek drainage and miles from her intended den site when the blue truck finally stopped near Kennedy Creek. This time, there were no gunshots, just the quiet click of an opening door and the muted beep of a radio signal. Only the forest talked as the first star poked through the sky and the day's melt soaked into the ground. Marta did not return to the den she had started.

A few days later, intrusions forgotten, she and Greatfoot were loafing along a different creek bed of the Ninemile. Sun poured in between the trees, trickles of water ran out from every last patch of snow, and the wolves were in a mood to run too. They dug up a cache of food and ate well on the thawed meat.

Marta was working on a leg bone, searching out the sweet marrow, when Greatfoot leaned over and pretended to snatch it from her. She clutched the bone between her bared teeth and rose, growling, then pranced past him, dragging the bone across the ground just out of reach. When Greatfoot pounced she swung the bone away, and the chase was on.

When Greatfoot tired of chasing Marta, Marta chased Greatfoot, and before long the bone was lost in the underbrush. On one downhill gallop Greatfoot ducked behind a thick bush, and Marta had sprinted out of sight before she realized the game had changed to hide-and-seek. They traded hiding places until they came to a road, where Marta cut loose in a joyous, full-out run. Together, Greatfoot and Marta ran into the forest and they ran across clear-cuts; they ran up creek beds and down ridges. They ran sunny loops and shady circles, feeling the land of the Ninemile grow familiar under their feet.

Finally thirsty and ready for a place to nap, the wolves dropped their pace. They ran side by side, with an occasional hip check from Marta or nip from Greatfoot, and circled around the edge of a clear cut, heading toward water. Marta crossed a ravine on a fallen log, and Greatfoot raced underneath, getting ahead and disappearing into the next ravine.

Coming over the rise, Marta peered cautiously around for her mate. But he wasn't hiding, waiting to pounce. He wasn't even looking at her. Greatfoot's head had disappeared into a hole: a fox den it seemed, the way his tail was twitching. Marta barked at her mate's behind, and he backed out of the hole.

The entrance was on the steep side of the ravine. Marta poked her nose inside. It was made by foxes, but no one was using it. She backed out and scratched at the dirt with her front foot. It was soft. She pawed with her other foot. The clay was damp, but dense. She sniffed and smelled the nearby creek. Suddenly her ears went forward, and she dug furiously with both paws, widening the hole in the side of the hill.

Playtime was over. It was time to make a home.

FORTY-FOUR

in the ninemile

Afew weeks later, in the foxhole she enlarged to a
wolf den, Marta gave birth to seven pups. All were
born healthy and strong except one. Shortly after the
birth, Greatfoot heard Marta whining piteously and crept
inside; at the mouth of the inner chamber, she had laid the
still-slick body of a dead pup. Delicately, he picked it up
in his great jaws and wriggled backward out of the den.
He trudged with it across the clear cut and up the ridge,
then buried the body under a cluster of young fir trees.

The Ninemile litter was twice as large as Marta's
first, and slowed her down more than twice as much. In
those first weeks, Greatfoot did all the killing. He
hunted farther and stronger than ever, and Marta kept
the pups well fed.

The den was near a road as well as the clear-cut, but

the logging was over, and few people had reason to come near. In the Ninemile, humans and cattle kept mostly to the valley bottom; the wolves, unless traveling, kept to the fringes and foothills around it. Inside the den, Marta sometimes heard the faint rumble of a truck through the clay walls, but the sound never came close enough to bother her. Except for Greatfoot's occasional run-in with a ranch dog, the wolves existed peacefully with their human neighbors in the Ninemile.

After a slow start, spring came easily to the Ninemile. By the time the first wildflowers had bloomed and faded, the six youngsters were out of the den and tumbling about the ravine. The pups grew quickly, and as before, their need for food grew with them. When they were ready for more than milk, Marta resumed hunting. She and Greatfoot took turns staying with the litter and bringing back meat, and though both were capable hunters, soon they were eating from, not adding to, their caches of food.

Hunting was only half the work. Keeping track of six wolf pups was a full-time enterprise, and the more the pups grew, the harder they were to contain. Sometimes Marta found herself dashing from one youngster to another, scolding with a short bark or the tips of her teeth, just to keep them safe in the ravine.

One day when Greatfoot was hunting, one of the

pups wandered from Marta's sight. Two of the others hadn't learned how to fight without hurting each other, so while the rest of the litter was playing with bones and sticks, Marta refereed Tenino and Camas. She let them wrestle, but separated them before they drew blood.

Tenino, a black female, was in a fierce mood, and Marta finally had to pull her off Camas before she did real damage. Nudging Tenino toward a meaty bone, Marta checked the others and found only three of them. Silver, a gray female, was missing. Hustling Tenino and Camas into the den, Marta plucked up the others and deposited them at the mouth of the hollow. She barked them all back into the darkness, then went looking for Silver.

At this age, a pup could not travel far. Marta followed Silver's scent up the ravine until she heard an ominous rush of wind and felt the wings of an owl beating the air above her. She stopped, holding her breath, and peered into the brightness overhead. There was no small gray shape in the owl's claws, and Marta let out her breath. But as she continued along her daughter's trail, the prey bird remained overhead.

Marta and the owl heard Silver's squeal at the same moment. The owl dived and the wolf lunged. The wolf had a tangle of bushes to go through, but the owl had farther to fall, and Marta reached Silver as the bird's talons opened. Instead of covering the pup, Marta attacked skyward, reaching up with her fangs. The owl was flailing just above Marta's head, stalled in its dive but not rising back into flight. Marta easily could have closed her jaws around the body of the bird, though not without a mouthful of talons and feathers. The wolf took a deep breath and roared. Silver closed her eyes at the sound, her attacker flapped free, and Marta closed her long teeth around air. Then she crouched over her daughter as owl droppings rained down through the trees.

Marta seized Silver by the neck and carried her back to the ravine. The other pups were clustered at the mouth of the den and came barreling forth when they saw their mother and sister. The youngsters mobbed Marta with puppy kisses and she dropped Silver to the ground, then sank down wearily in the shelter of the ravine. The youngsters tumbled over one another to get to her milk. When Greatfoot returned, sides bulging from the hunt, such was the scene that greeted him: Marta asleep, heaped over with pups, each one breathing steady and warm.

At their father's arrival, the heap of pups sprang to life. Greatfoot smelled richly, but before the youngsters could storm him with their begging, into their midst stepped Marta. Knee deep in pups, she reached for her mate's muzzle and closed her great jaws lightly around it. Greatfoot blinked at the feel of her pointed teeth on his soft, whiskered cheeks.

As he stepped away to unload his cargo of meat, a song began low in Marta's chest. She tipped back her head and one by one, six little heads also tipped back; she sang, and they joined in. It was the coming-home howl, and they sang until Greatfoot had emptied his belly. Then he, too, joined in.

When she finally lowered her head, Marta saw what she had seen once before, only in a dream, during her long sleep on the shore of Flathead Lake. Now the dream unfolded around her. The strange valley was the Ninemile; the strange pack was her own; and the great, looping tracks in the golden clay around the den belonged to her mate. Marta was home.

PART FOUR

FORTY-FIVE

another noise

From the moment the pups were allowed outside the den, it was clear that Silver liked to run as much as her elders did. She was also the leader of the litter, so when she took off, others tried to follow. Soon after Silver's encounter with the owl, it became impossible to keep the pups together in the ravine, and the time had come for the pack to move to its first rendezvous site. Marta left the youngsters with Greatfoot and went on a mission.

In part, her mission was to move: to stretch, to run, to feel the earth moving underneath her feet. In part, it was to hunt: the meat from Greatfoot's last kill was gone, the food caches were nearly exhausted, and the pups' appetites were growing like meadow grass. With luck, she would be able to make a kill near a good rendezvous site and lead the pack to it.

Spring was turning to summer. Except for her recent hunts, Marta had been confined in the den and ravine, and she was eager to travel. She took off eastward, toward the sun and Kennedy Creek, with a bright bound that matched the brightness of the day.

At the den, Greatfoot gnawed patiently on the ball end of a deer bone as he watched the pups dig in the clay, play tug-of-war with sinew or bark, and wrestle. Twice he had to separate Tenino and Camas, and several times he marched off to collect Silver, who was no longer content to chew sticks and chase grasshoppers. Punctuated by Greatfoot's lessons, the morning disappeared in a rhythm of play and napping, nap and playing, and slowly turned to afternoon. The weather changed with the day, and what had been a golden, spicy morning became a tense and gritty afternoon. The sky crusted over with gray—a cold, hard color—and the birds that had been out collecting food for nestlings settled into silence.

It was too late for a spring blizzard, but the mood overhead was one of threat, not promise. The pups gathered close to Greatfoot as the weather changed, and when the first drops began to pelt, he nudged some and carried others into the den. Silver ran in on her own. The youngsters were old enough to be out in the rain—they had already frolicked in one spring storm—but this smelled like hail.

The first lightning struck moments after the pack took to its shelter. Marta had not returned and the pups were hungry, so Greatfoot dashed out to the nearest cache, dug up the last of the meat, and brought it back to the youngsters. They fell upon it like lost souls, chewing hard with their pointed milk teeth, and looking surprised when a mouthful proved hard to swallow.

Outside, the storm raged and fumed. Hail fell like bullets, and one sharp crack after another pierced the air. A tree fell with a great snap in the direction of Kennedy Creek. At each new sound the pups looked up from their chewing to see whether they should be afraid, but Greatfoot sat calmly at the entrance to the inner chamber, his profile outlined in the gray light from outside.

Finally the thunderstorm began to subside. The last balls of hail popped onto the flat grasses, and the sky brightened with the promise of sunset. Cracks of thunder rolled across the heavens behind the storm, and one final shot sounded in the next drainage. As the weather calmed, the pups dropped off to sleep, all except Timber, one of the gray males. Timber was too hungry to sleep— he still preferred milk to meat—and sat with Greatfoot at the entrance, waiting for the sun and Marta's return.

The sun came, but Marta did not. A fiery sunset

spread across the Ninemile, and the birds resumed their peeping. Greatfoot wriggled out of the den with Timber close behind. A large gray shape, stepping gracefully, followed by a small gray shape that tottered and tumbled, made its way from the ravine to the edge of the clear-cut. They stood silently as lightning bolts spiked out of the red-edged clouds, and suddenly Greatfoot howled. He reared back and called Marta with a cry that echoed off the Ninemile peaks. Timber howled too, but his little voice drowned in the storm of his father's. Greatfoot's call was wide and long, aimed to find his mate wherever she had holed up from the storm. There was no reply.

Greatfoot howled again, Timber beside him. Again no reply.

As the last tinges of red dissolved from the sky, the deep wolf call sounded again and again across the Nine-mile Valley. The only response was the fading rumble of the away-going storm.

FORTY-SIX

no sign

Marta never returned. Greatfoot called and called, but she did not answer.

Just as Marta had searched for Calef, Greatfoot searched for Marta. That night, leaving the pups in the den with an abrupt bark, he left and followed her tracks. Her path zigged and zagged along the usual trails until it crossed the Kennedy Creek road. There it vanished. There was no blood, no fur, no sign of struggle. No sign.

The forest was silent.

Greatfoot was silent. A heaviness weighed on the land, as though each sprig of green around him struggled to hold the sky in place. Greatfoot sniffed once at the place where Marta's footprints vanished. A boot mark pressed into the wet clay. There was a car track.

Greatfoot did not sniff it. He stood and did not move for a very long time.

When he moved a howl rose from the center of his belly, but his throat closed around it. No sound would come out.

FORTY-SEVEN

greatfoot hunts

Marta was gone, and Greatfoot was alone with the pups. He was more alone than Marta had been without Calef, having no packmates—not even a wise one with broken teeth—to help raise the litter. Greatfoot's alpha instinct rose. He hunted with twice his usual vigor and ran with twice the speed, and his success was great. But it did not bring Marta back.

Nothing could bring Marta back. Like the winter snow that had vanished from the Ninemile, she too had disappeared. Greatfoot hunted for her; he hunted the hills and lowlands near the den, but when he smelled her sign, it was old sign; when he found her tracks, they were old tracks, usually mixed with his, all made before the day of the storm.

Greatfoot could not find Marta because she was not

there to be found. The poacher who took her life also took her body, leaving only her radio collar—leather cut, transmitter smashed—submerged in Kennedy Creek. The merest hint of Marta's scent rose from the creek bubbles there, too faint to be found even by her mate's great nose.

As the sole provider for the new litter, Greatfoot had at least one shortcoming: he could not turn meat to milk. The pups were almost ready to be weaned, and though Greatfoot could hunt all the meat they could eat, they could not eat much with their baby teeth. Wanting to nurse, Silver attacked Greatfoot's belly, protesting when she found his nipples hard and dry. When Greatfoot snapped at her the other pups stood back, perplexed—but stayed away from their father's belly.

With his next kill, Greatfoot moved the pack to a rendezvous site. Not far from the den, it was on a logging road that had been gated shut, and no traffic came through. The clearing had water and surrounding trees for cover; the grass was thick with mice and moles that made good practice for beginning hunters.

After Marta's disappearance, the pups changed in different ways. Tenino grew tense and high-strung while Chinook, the other black female, became timid and withdrawn. Timber and Camas, the gray males, wrestled constantly. Silver remained the leader, getting the most and best of everything. Even so, she sometimes stood alone at the edge of the rendezvous site and crooned, a quiet howl sung only to the forest. Blackfeet, the black male, became a full-time hunter. While the others lost weight, Blackfeet fed himself on a steady diet of small animals and even insects.

Greatfoot was on the run. It was not his usual joyous running, but a desperate, hungry pace that left him increasingly thin and tired. He slept hard and played little, but even as his body ran down, his alpha blood ran strong. Asleep or awake, when the pups begged for food, he responded. Greatfoot became a creature of one purpose, with a single search image in his head: the whitetail deer. He let nothing get in his way.

There was little to get in his way except the dogs who sometimes harassed him as he came and went across the Ninemile. The harder he hunted, the less patience he had for these not-quite-wolves. One night, returning from a hunt that had taken him across the freeway and into the Idaho forest, Greatfoot was pulled off course by the insistent barking of a ranch dog.

Many times he had ignored such an uproar. Tonight he was foot sore and meat drunk, and his belly was stretched agonizingly full with food for the pups. Veering off his path to the rendezvous site, Greatfoot turned onto the ranch and shouldered through a herd of cattle toward the dog.

The closer Greatfoot came, the louder the dog barked and the more confused its message became. The dog was protecting his territory and expected Greatfoot—as the intruder—to back down. But its bark said nothing about territory to Greatfoot. As the alpha wolf in his territory, he expected the smaller animal to back down, and he leaped the fence where the dog was contained. When the wolf finally faced the dog, still barking, he charged.

Blood-mad at the tangle of canine and human scent, Greatfoot attacked. The two snapped and bit at each other—sometimes connecting, sometimes not. Suddenly Greatfoot stopped and raised his head: there was a vehicle coming down the road. The wolf leaped back over the fence, leaving the dog licking its wounds, and bolted past the cow herd.

Still weighed down by meat, he barely cleared the barbwire fence, and it made a bloody gouge in the skin of his belly. As Greatfoot disappeared into the woods below the rendezvous site, a pickup truck bumped slowly past the ranch, raising a cloud of dust in its taillights. The dark-blue color of the truck blended into the night, but the low, clear rumble was the same as ever.

FORTY-EIGHT

the way of the wolf

Being hungry and half orphaned was not enough to keep wolf pups from their job of growing up. There were games to be played, bones to be chewed, races to run, and wolf ways to learn. The rendezvous site was the scene of at least one ongoing boxing match, interrupted by greedy feasts when Greatfoot reappeared, and long naps in between.

In time, all the pups adjusted to their milk-less diet as Blackfeet had, and slowly began to put on weight. Few wolves could have brought back enough food to keep six pups alive, but few wolves were Greatfoot. The many deer in the Ninemile, and in the forests stretching in many directions, made it possible. With Marta, survival would have been easy. Without her, it was a daily struggle.

In the time after his mate disappeared, Greatfoot ran on instinct: travel, hunt, feed; travel, hunt, feed. Sleep, and begin again. As the pups grew, he moved from one rendezvous site to the next. At first he had to carry them one by one, making six trips to complete the move; later they were able to run along on their own, a ragtag band led by Silver. At the new place, they were usually greeted by a fresh kill their father had made.

The pups had learned the game of follow the leader before they ever left the den, and from Greatfoot they slowly gathered their first wolf ways. Watching him, their instincts took shape. They learned the faces and postures of wolf language; they learned to chase and hide, and to track and hunt small animals. They learned the many howls: the hungry howl, the lonesome howl, the hunting howl, the feasting howl. They learned the howl that called their father, and the howl he used to call them.

And they learned to avoid things human. Following Greatfoot, they hid from the sound of cars and side-stepped the tracks of horses. They learned how to slip through a herd of cattle without causing a stir, and they learned to keep their distance from the people and dogs of the Ninemile.

One human scent was hard to avoid. This one did not stay to the valley bottom, but walked the paths the wolves walked. From one rendezvous to the next, and sometimes in between, the scent came before or followed after them. No person ever appeared with it, though sometimes in the quiet, the pack could hear the rumble of a truck driving slowly along the logging roads. When it brought no threat, Greatfoot no longer ran from the sound, and neither did the pups.

By the end of summer, the young wolves were ready to go along on short hunts. The hunt was the heart of wolf ways, and when the pack had learned it, Greatfoot would no longer have to hunt alone. But first, he had to teach them stealth. To a pack of six young wolves, everything was a game, the noisier the better. On their first hunt Blackfeet picked up Greatfoot's silence, but the others were too excited. Greatfoot had to sprint ahead, leaving the noise behind, to get near any deer.

After several tries he finally felled an old buck. Blackfeet was close enough to see how the strike was made, and by the time the deer was on the ground, the swarm of five had caught up. Though they didn't see the attack, they had the feel for the chase, and they quickly understood what to do next. After Greatfoot ripped open the belly of the deer, the pack leaped around him. The pups still didn't have the right teeth for tearing hide or breaking bones, but with Greatfoot's help, they got a share of meat. Soon the area was littered with small debris: parts of bone, fur, strips of meat and even fat were scattered around. This would be their new rendezvous.

Even after the pups began to tag along on short hunts, Greatfoot still traveled alone to get most of their food. He would leave the pack together at a rendezvous site and hunt through the night. Often he traveled great distances, returning by morning with a belly full of fresh meat.

On the night when the first frost collected in the Ninemile, Greatfoot was away on a hunt. The pups wakened to find the ground glittering in sunlight. Silver rose first, shaking sparkles from her coat, and raced around the rendezvous site to get warm. This roused the others, and soon the litter was up and exploring the frosty clearing. They amused themselves with scraps from the earlier kill, played raven tag with the birds hovering around, and waited for Greatfoot to return with their food.

Midday came, and Greatfoot had not arrived. By early afternoon Blackfeet was chasing rabbits, and his brothers and sisters were picking at the carcass along with the ravens. Silver left the rendezvous site and wandered into the forest. She howled once and stood for a moment, listening, then went sniffing for food caches and hunting in a halfhearted way.

By nightfall Greatfoot had still not returned, and the pups began to sing. They sang the hungry song and the calling song; they sang the lonely song and the cold song. There was no answer. They went to sleep as they had wakened, frosted and curled against one another for warmth.

Greatfoot did not return the next morning, or the one after that. The pups stayed close to the rendezvous site, and as the sun dragged across the sky, they played less and slept more. They picked the deer carcass clean and chased rabbits into the forest. Except for Blackfeet, they did not try to hunt without Greatfoot. Stomachs grumbling, they howled for him at dawn and dark. Then, on the evening of the third day, their call was answered.

It was not their father's voice, but it was a kind of wolf call, and the pups raced toward it. They left the rendezvous site and streaked through the trees, following the howl to the edge of the valley. They reached a logging road and the howl trailed off, but by then Silver had picked up the scent of food. They followed her off the road and into an unused cattle pasture. Just out of sight of the road, whole and untouched, lay a dead deer.

Greatfoot was nowhere to be seen. Sniffing ecstatically at the deer's mouth and belly, the pups were too hungry to notice that his scent was missing, too. In its place was a trace of human scent: the familiar smell of the person they no longer bothered to run from. The pups ignored it, crowding around the carcass. There were no openings in the hide, and Greatfoot was not there to show them where to begin. Silver tugged hopefully at a leg, which sprang back stiffly and did not give. Tenino bit at the bile-covered tongue, but it was tough and firmly attached. Timber and Camas tried to chew through the fur, but it was too thick for their new teeth. Blackfeet stood apart, cocked his head, and whined; while the others clustered in confusion around the deer, he watched.

Unable to get at the meat, the young wolves returned hungry to the rendezvous site. Still Greatfoot did not appear, and Tenino grew anxious. She raced around the rendezvous site, howling and whining, and chewed nervously at her paws. That night, as the other pack members rested, she stayed awake. She paced back and forth in the cooling air, stopping near her sleeping packmates and sniffing at the last scent marks, now days old, left by their father.

In the stillness, she heard a familiar rumble in the distance. She pricked her ears toward the sound and heard the quiet scrape of rubber tires on the logging road, in the direction of the deer they had found. The sound stopped, and the valley was silent again.

Standing next to Silver, Tenino sighed and lay down. Resting her chin on Silver's shoulders, the black wolf finally closed her eyes and accepted sleep. None of the wolves heard the distant rumble or scrape as the pickup truck started again, moving quietly off into the night.

FORTY-NINE

the gift

The next morning, the wolves went out to investigate the deer carcass. It lay in the same position, but the belly had been sliced neatly open.

Ravens had gotten there first and were plucking at the entrails when the pack arrived. The wolves chased off the ravens and dove ferociously for the insides. They started with the organs that were easiest to chew, but when the cavity was empty they still were not full. Timber and Camas had the best teeth, and they attacked the hide as they had seen Greatfoot do, pulling it back to expose the meat underneath.

Unlike other kills, this deer didn't move much when they pulled at it. One leg was chained to the ground and held firm when they tugged and tore at the carcass. Blackfeet sniffed nervously at the chain, but soon gave in to the smell of fresh meat. They feasted in wolf style, Silver fighting Camas for the best pieces, and Chinook taking tidbits lost in the others' contest. Their meal lasted all morning, and when the sun was high and they were finally full, the deer carcass was mostly bones.

The wolves rested and cleaned themselves. Silver and Chinook napped, Blackfeet and Camas chewed on leg bones, and Tenino and Timber played raven tag with the birds. It was an ordinary scene, except for one thing: this pack had no leader.

No matter how long the pups waited or how often they called, they could not bring Greatfoot back because he had been killed on his last hunt. The freeway he crossed to and from the Idaho forest ran fast with cars and trucks, and he often had to wait for an opening in the traffic. The last time Greatfoot was crossing the highway back from the hunt, heavy with food for the pups, a pair of headlights came at him unexpectedly. Meat-drunk and tired, the wolf could not move out of the way quickly enough; the driver swerved, but not soon enough.

For the orphaned pack, the gift of food came just in time. Revived, they returned to the rendezvous site and took up their routine of playing, fighting, and hunting. Throughout that day and night the pups continued to call for Greatfoot, but he did not appear. After dark, the blue truck cruised slowly along the road behind their rendezvous site, then disappeared into the night. Later, in the distance, the wolves received another answer to their calls: a wolflike howl, deep and warm, but again it was not their father's. Last time, this song had brought food. The pups howled to it, and it howled back.

The next morning, when the wolves went to pick over their deer bones, they found more than ravens. In place of the bones was another freshly killed deer.

The scene repeated itself for weeks. Every few days, the bones of the last kill would disappear and a new one would appear in its place. The pack called back and forth with the distant voice, but never saw or smelled another wolf. The blue pickup came and went, and traces of human scent appeared with the kills, but no person ever came near enough to be seen or heard.

When fall settled over the Ninemile, the young wolves tried to learn wolf ways on their own. As they grew stronger and bigger, like Blackfeet they learned to chase and hunt their share of small animals. They grew adept at hunting rabbits alone and sometimes tracked a deer in twos and threes, but without Greatfoot, their learning was slow and haphazard.

Hunting season came to the Ninemile, bringing an explosion of gunfire and traffic that sent the wolves scrambling for shelter. At night when the blasts ended and the traffic trickled away, the pack moved cautiously about. Silver was first to discover the gut piles left by hunters. She howled with surprise, and her brothers and sisters came running. They gobbled up the vitals, licked their chops, and exchanged happy, sloppy wolf kisses.

Throughout hunting season, every few mornings the wolves discovered a new carcass at the usual place. Rabbits and hunters' leavings filled the gaps in their growing bellies, but it was the gift of the deer that sustained them. Physically the pack grew strong, but the pups were still too young to be without a leader. They had wolf bodies and wolf instinct, but without wolf elders, they could not learn true wolf ways.

The pack survived in its own ways. Hunger taught them to hunt, and the meals of deer kept their taste for wild meat. A kind of order developed among the pups, with Silver at one end and Chinook at the other. As the weather grew cold, their hunger grew with it, and soon they were tracking and chasing deer as a pack.

Sometimes they saw the blue truck, but only when it was parked silently on the road; more often they heard it moving through the night, going to and from the pasture where they found the deer. They stopped calling for Greatfoot, but whenever the mysterious howls sounded across the valley, the orphaned pack answered. It was not their father's song, but to them it meant survival.

FIFTY

the man

One night in the middle of hunting season, the call seemed to come from closer than usual. Silver's ears went up, and instead of singing with the rest of the pack, she ran to the edge of the rendezvous site. When Blackfeet slipped around her into the woods she followed, and the gray and black wolves crept cautiously toward the sound. The others finished their howl one by one and joined the line slipping through the woods. When the voice was silent, the wolves stopped and called. The howls kept coming from the same place. They were getting closer.

The pack of youngsters crept stealthily toward the sound, which came from somewhere beyond the chained deer carcass. They could not see or smell a wolf anywhere in the darkness, just a hint of the human scent they already knew. The voice seemed to be coming from behind a hillock, and the young pack fanned out as it had once done on hunts with Greatfoot, closing in on the rise from all sides.

The closer they got, the slower they crept. Still the calls came.

All six reached the hillock at the same time. One last call sounded from behind it, but this time, they did not answer. They peered over the rise, and what they saw was not a wolf at all.

Crouched in the cold, damp grass behind the rise was a man. Breath steaming, hands cupped around his mouth for the next howl, he saw the faces surrounding him and slowly lowered his hands. The wolves looked at the man. The man looked at the wolves.

Seven hearts pounded in seven chests, and seven pairs of eyes grew wide. This was not a stranger, not their leader, not any wolf at all—and neither was it their enemy. This was one who had called to them, who had fed them, who had watched over them when first Marta, then Greatfoot, disappeared.

For one moment, wolf eyes and human eyes met. Then six tails turned with a bound, a leap, a scramble and a flash, and were gone. When the man finally stood in the darkness, he could see only one black and one gray shape. Well out of reach and almost out of sight, Black-feet and Silver had stopped and turned, pausing to look back at him.

The man howled again. As his tones dissolved into the night the two wolves stood, still watching, still silent. The man held his breath and did not move. First Silver and then Blackfeet gathered their feet and raced off into the blackness. A faint tatter on fallen leaves, and all was silent. The man listened, then let out his breath and turned toward the blue truck waiting on the road.

As he took the first step away from the hillock, the call came from behind him. Blackfeet. Then Silver. Then Tenino and Timber and Camas and Chinook. The pack sang, from where each stood in the forest, breath rising into the frosted air. Wolves were home in the Ninemile.

epilogue

The wolf I call Marta did live, much in the manner recorded here. Most of what is known about her life comes from records kept by the U.S. Fish and Wildlife Service and used in the federal wolf recovery effort. The major events of this story and many of the details about the animals came directly from those records. The day-to-day details that cannot be known were filled in from studies and stories of wolf behavior and ecology.

As the documents show, the Pleasant Valley pack had formed in northwest Montana by the spring of 1989. That April the alpha male, whom I call Calef, was killed by a sheep rancher who mistook him for a dog. In the next months the remaining wolves were suspected of cattle deaths in the area, though other causes were later found. Nonetheless, the decision was made to relocate the pack. Except for one black pup who avoided capture, the wolves were trapped, darted, kenneled, then held in the Ashley Creek Animal Clinic in Kalispell while awaiting transport to a site in the Bob Marshall Wilderness complex. In an eleventh-hour decision after the wolves were already sedated, Governor Stan Stephens halted the transfer, and the destination was changed to Nyack Creek in Glacier Park.

After relocation, Marta's radio collar allowed biologists to follow her travels through the Swan and Mission mountains. She met the male I call Greatfoot that winter, and the first Ninemile pups were born in the spring of 1990. Marta disappeared over Memorial Day, not long after the litter was born. After weeks of searching by authorities, a fisherman discovered Marta's collar, transmitter smashed, in Kennedy Creek. Her body was never found.

As Marta lived, so did her packmates. All the wolves named in this book were real animals identified by recovery biologists. Annie and Sula both died of starvation in Glacier Park, and Oldtooth, disabled by his foot injury, was caught preying on livestock and euthanized. Greatfoot raised the six Ninemile pups successfully over the summer, but three months after Marta's death, on Labor Day weekend, he was hit by a car while crossing the freeway west of Missoula. Wildlife biologist Mike

Jimenez, who had been monitoring the pack, fed the orphaned pups with roadkill; his face-to-face encounter with the young wolves is recorded in the last chapter of the book.

After Thanksgiving, Mike discontinued the feeding in hopes that the pups would learn to hunt for themselves. They did. Even so, the young Ninemile pack did not fare well after the deaths of its leaders. Pikuni separated from the pack first, and Silver soon after. The remaining four were found killing livestock on the far side of Reservation Divide and, in the spring of 1991, were captured for relocation to Glacier Park. Camas came out of the drug early and escaped, but Tenino, Chinook, and Timber were released in Glacier and traveled together for a time before splitting up.

Eventually, Chinook was shot and killed for attacking cattle near Dixon; Timber was killed illegally and found in a lake near Bigfork; Tenino remained on the east side of the Continental Divide but was captured there after killing two lambs and sent to Wolf Haven in Washington State.

Of the other wolves, they or their offspring may still be at large. Rann's fate remains, happily, unknown; for a time there were reports in Pleasant Valley of a smaller black wolf traveling with a larger gray wolf, so perhaps he found a friend and mentor. Silver, Pikuni, and Camas are likewise unaccounted for. I like to think they are free somewhere, perhaps in the Ninemile, perhaps in Idaho, or perhaps in one of the other valleys newly inhabited by wolf packs.

Though the deaths of so many wolves make this story tragic, for their species it ends with hope. Marta did for the Ninemile Valley what the federal government has done in Yellowstone National Park: return wolves to the habitat from which they were removed, often forcibly and by extreme measures, during the last hundred years. The return of the wolf is a natural process that takes place as a population outgrows its territory, and individuals disperse to new and sometimes distant places; wildlife biologist Diane Boyd has studied the process in detail. Natural wolf recovery depends on the tenacity of these pioneer wolves and the tolerance of humans in areas where they settle.

Because Marta was by all accounts tenacious, and her neighbors relatively tolerant, she and her packmates were successful in their journey home. The Ninemile Valley continues to be occupied by packs of varying size, and dozens of pups have been raised to adulthood. Chances are good that Marta and Greatfoot's bloodline is still present there. In a haunting footnote, Mike Jimenez told me that the fate of Marta and Greatfoot was repeated in excruciating detail in the summer of 1995, when the alpha female of the Ninemile pack was killed illegally, and the male was hit on the freeway. However, this time the pack included other adults, so the young of the year were not entirely alone.

Despite such setbacks, the frontier Marta pushed forward has been expanding. In addition to the long-standing Camas wolves of Glacier Park and the new inhabitants of Yellowstone, resident wolves are now making their home in Montana, Idaho, Wyoming, and other regions of the northern Rockies. This ecosystem was wolf country long before it was claimed by humans; if the habitat is preserved and wolf populations are allowed to recover, our two species may share this extraordinary place for ages to come.

author's statement

When this story came to me, I was not a wolf person. I was an author who worked in writing, broadcasting, and education. I did have a fascination for wilderness that developed after I moved to Montana in my twenties; it led me to write *The Huckleberry Book*, and I often touched on natural resource issues in my newspaper column. At the time, however, I was neither a wildlife biologist nor an animal tracker, and as an outdoorswoman I was more enthusiastic than accomplished.

Like many of my neighbors in northwest Montana, I had followed the story of the Pleasant Valley wolves in the *Daily InterLake*. One day after work in June of 1991, I found myself reading about yet another wolf death: the body of one of the Ninemile pups, a yearling, had been found floating in Mud Lake, not far from my home in Flathead County. Like too many others, the Mud Lake killing was not accidental. For me, it was one death too many.

The book formed itself in that moment, as I stood looking at the newspaper. This was a story that needed to be told. It had to be told from the wolves' perspective, it had to be true to the facts that were known, and it had to be accessible to young people. I did not know where the story would begin or end, or who its heroes would be; I did not know what it would take to make science dramatic and drama scientific; at that moment, I scarcely knew the difference between a wolf and a coyote. There was much I had to learn.

Over the next four years, I did that learning. Between graduate school, teaching, and writing projects, I walked the mountains these wolves walked; I studied wolf science; I interviewed wildlife biologists; I studied maps and drew diagrams; I played with captive pups and had my coffee cup stolen by a quick-witted mom. As I learned, I wrote: badly at first, but better as I learned the ways of the wolf, the lives of these wolves, and the shape of their story. Slowly the book came into being.

Though this story belongs to the wolves, its existence in book form would not have been possible without the help of many human beings. Wolves seem to inspire a measure of generosity, patience, and courage in our species, and this book has been the beneficiary of that.

For science, I thank Mike Jimenez, Joe Fontaine, Diane Boyd, Carter Neimeyer, Steve Fritts, Mike Fairchild, and books by L. David Mech. For the opportunity to observe live wolves, I am beholden to the Triple D Game Farm. For editing assistance, I am grateful to Alex McLennon (and Savana), Jack Campbell, Hillary Funk, Maggie Jimenez, and the insightful others who read the manuscript at crucial stages. To those friends who variously accompanied me, saved me, sheltered me, hiked in to meet me on (and sometimes wisely talked me out of) those long wolf excursions, I owe you. For the previous edition of this book, my thanks to Michael Korda of Simon and Schuster. For the volume you now hold, all credit goes to my editor Melanie Cecka; my agent, Charlotte Sheedy; and the "godmother" who brought us together, attorney Karen Shatzkin. Finally, for living the story it has been my privilege to write: the wolves.

After all my research, I still am not a wolf scientist—that title is long in the earning—but I have come to see the world in a new way. I have tried to see it through wild eyes, to smell and feel it through wild nose and paws, and to love it with a wild heart.

To see the world through wolf eyes is not so great a leap as it may seem. Our two species have much in common with each other. We are intelligent, adaptable animals who work and play with a passion; we form complex and enduring social bonds; we share a sometimes-fragile environment; we love to sing.

There are important differences. Where humans adapt the environment to meet our needs, the wolf must adapt to the environment and so, like other animals, belongs to nature in a way we can only imagine. The wolf is not just a symbol of wildness; the wolf is wildness. We cannot live in nature as she does, but we can—with a little imagination and a little more effort—walk to the edge of our world, and peer over the edge into hers.

The wolf is a spark of nature's intelligence that lives apart from, and sometimes despite, the structure of houses and cars and jobs around which our lives are now built. In her freedom, she reminds us of the wild spark from which we came, and to which we all, in the end, return.